MORE THAN A MEMORY

Lois Faye Dyer

A KISMET™ Romance

METEOR PUBLISHING CORPORATION
Bensalem, Pennsylvania

First Printing April 1992.

ISBN: 1-56597-003-9

Printed in the United States of America

With special thanks to my husband, Bud, for sharing with me his memories of racing with the gang from Pettigrew Muffler in Oxnard, California.

LOIS FAYE DYER

Winner of the 1989–1990 Romantic Times Reviewer's Choice Award for Best New Series Author, Lois Faye Dyer lives on Washington State's beautiful Puget Sound with her husband, two children, and their irascible parrot, Dylan. She ended a career as a paralegal and Superior Court Clerk to fulfill a lifelong dream to write and when she's not involved in writing, she enjoys long walks on the beach with her husband, watching musical and western movies from the 1940's and 1950's and, most of all, indulging her passionate addiction to reading.

Other books by Lois Faye Dyer:

No. 4 *WINTERFIRE*
No. 21 *THAT JAMES BOY*
No. 70 *SUNDAY KIND OF LOVE*

ONE

"You still look a bit stunned, Cole," Sarah teased, blue eyes twinkling as they observed her oldest brother. It was easy to see that the two were related, for there was a marked family resemblance in their high cheekbones, thick-lashed blue eyes, and blonde hair. Cole's tall, broad-shouldered body and handsome, strong-boned face were aggressively masculine versions of Sarah's slender feminine curves and softer features.

"I *am* stunned," Cole answered promptly, a lazy smile curving the hard line of his mouth as he returned her affectionate gaze. He shook his head in disbelief. "It's still hard to believe that my baby sister is going to have a baby of her own."

Sarah's husband grinned and dropped a possessive kiss on the end of her nose.

"*She*," Jesse said proudly. "We're having a girl."

Cole nodded, blue eyes faintly bemused as he looked at the two.

"Yeah, I know. Mom told me," he eyed Jesse as his black-haired brother-in-law dropped another kiss against Sarah's cheek and returned to slicing his steak. "Damned if you don't look like a typical proud papa, Jesse!"

"I *am* a typical proud father, Cole."

The two men exchanged a look that satisfied Cole's protective instincts and silence reigned for a few moments while the three concentrated on their dinner. Around them, the hum of conversation and laughter from neighboring tables ebbed and flowed, accompanied by the clink of silver and glassware.

The Lakeshore Supper Club was a popular spot with both tourists and local CastleRock, Iowa, residents and even on this Wednesday night the round tables were filled. Long French doors were opened wide onto the club's broad veranda and a faint breeze teased the surface of the lake waters and drifted into the dining room, carrying the sweet scent of summer roses and blooming lilacs.

Cole glanced around the familiar room. It had been the site of McFadden family celebrations for as long as he could remember. Only eighteen months ago, Jesse and Sarah's reception had been held here, a wedding Cole couldn't attend because he'd been racing that weekend. He'd missed so many special occasions, he reflected somberly. Success and fame had exacted a high price.

He rubbed the aching muscles in his thigh with an absent-minded motion that had become almost an unnoticed habit in the last few weeks. If it weren't for the crash that had damaged his leg and forced him to leave the circuit to recuperate, he would have been in Darlington again this week. The grueling physical exercises he'd forced his body to endure had strengthened his leg, although he knew it would be weeks yet before it could withstand the physical strain of a NASCAR race. But after six weeks of hospitalization and the last two weeks prowling around his parents' home, he was restless and bored with the forced inactivity.

He sipped his wine and contemplated the couple across the table from him. It was easy to see they were happy together; Sarah positively glowed when she looked at her husband and contentment lay deep in Jesse's green eyes. Cole loved his little sister and he'd known and liked Jesse for years; he was happy for them. He pushed away a faint, rare tug of wistful longing as he watched them. He'd chosen a career over a settled family life long, long ago. Their kind of married bliss wasn't for him, and he knew it. So why did he feel this unsettled longing for a dream never realized and this aching, deep sadness for what could never be?

He shifted restlessly as he grimly acknowledged the truth. It wasn't just seeing Sarah and Jesse together that tapped the old sadness buried deep within him. It was also, in large part, returning to CastleRock with its memories that were better left unstirred. It was the sultry heat of the Iowa summer night and the heavy scent of summer roses underlaid with the faint, distinctive flavor of lakewater that resurrected memories of long-ago August nights and the black-haired, green-eyed seductress who had stolen his heart.

Cole grimaced and swallowed the rest of his wine. If there was one thing he'd learned in the last eight years, it was that grieving for might-have-beens brought only pain and useless regrets. He glanced idly around the supper club once again, his blue gaze flicking casually over the couple standing in the entry, then drifting on before something familiar about the slender line of the woman's back, as she stood half-turned away from the room and spoke to her companion, drew his attention back to her. Ebony hair fell in a silky mane halfway down the enticing curve of her spine, the ends curling neatly under to brush against the smooth, tanned skin of her shoulder blades, bare above the low neckline of her green summer evening dress.

Narrow-eyed, Cole held his breath, forgetting to breathe while he willed her to turn around so that he could see her face. As if hearing his silent command, she obeyed. Cole's heart stopped beating, joining his lungs in their inability to function as he stared at the face that had haunted his nights and tormented his days for the last eight years.

"Good evening, Miss Winters, Mr. Bateman. Table for two this evening?"

Melanie Winters brushed a strand of blue-black

hair back over her shoulder and smiled warmly at the young hostess.

"Yes, please," Eric answered for them, stepping aside to let her follow the girl as she threaded her way among the white linen-covered tables to the far side of the room. Melanie placed her green silk evening bag on the snowy tablecloth next to her napkin and sank gratefully into a chair.

"Thank you, Tiffany," she said as she accepted a gold-tasseled menu from the hostess. "How are you enjoying your summer?"

Cole watched intently as she smiled up at the young girl and chatted. She was as heartwrenchingly lovely as his memories. Her mane of silky ebony hair was pulled back from her temples and caught up on the crown of her head with gold combs. The delicate shells of her ears were framed by the thick sheaf of hair that fell down her back. Beneath the green silk sundress, her body was high-breasted, tiny-waisted and long-legged, the off-the-shoulder, backless dress exposing satiny, sun-kissed skin.

Her back was to him but when she turned to speak to her escort, Cole could see her profile with its fine-boned, delicate nose and the stubborn little chin, the lush curve of her lips, the long sweep of black lashes. The only jewelry she wore were small gold hoops in her ears, and a thin gold chain on her left wrist that matched the narrow-linked chain around her neck. A surge of relief loosened taut muscles as his searching gaze found no ring on the third finger of her left hand when she handed the menu back to the young girl.

"Cole? Cole—?" Sarah's perplexed voice intruded on his concentration and he forced his gaze away from the couple across the room. Sarah was staring at him and as his eyes finally met hers, she looked past him to study the other table and its occupants. She knew the man only slightly, but the woman with him was a dear friend and her face softened with warm affection as her gaze ran over Melanie's profile before she turned back to Cole. "You haven't heard a word I've said!" she teased, wondering at the tension visible in his set face. "What is it? You look like you've seen a ghost!"

Cole winced visibly. Sarah had no idea how close to the bone her comment cut.

"No—not a ghost," he said roughly, pouring another glass of wine. "Just someone I used to know."

Sarah frowned and her gaze sought out Melanie and her escort.

"Melanie Winters? I didn't know you knew her."

"I knew her once—but it was a long time ago." He shrugged as if it was unimportant but tension still gripped his hard body. "Is that her husband she's with?"

"No, she's not married. That's Eric Bateman. He's the high-school principal. He and Melanie have dated fairly steadily for the last few years, but as far as I know, they aren't considering marriage."

Cole was only slightly relieved to confirm that she wasn't married. It sounded as if she and Bateman were an acknowledged couple.

"Melanie managed to get us through our wedding without either of us having heart failure," Jesse commented. "I don't think anyone else could have coped with Sarah's lists and paranoia over details!"

Sarah tilted her chin and sniffed at the teasing glance he slanted her.

"I am not paranoid! If it hadn't been for my lists and Melanie's help with planning the wedding, I would never have gotten all the arrangements done in time."

"You're right, sweetheart," Jesse brushed an affectionate kiss against her temple. "And I'm eternally thankful that you hired a wedding consultant—Melanie was great."

Cole frowned in confusion. "Is that what Melanie does? Plan weddings?"

"Yes, she's a bridal consultant," Sarah answered, her gaze warm with shared memories as she met Jesse's green eyes. "And she also owns a womenswear shop in town that carries bridal gowns and lingerie."

"What's the name of her shop, honey?" Jesse asked.

"Victoria's Garden," she answered promptly.

"Oh, yeah," a wicked grin spread across his dark features, "that's where you bought that little silk—"

"Never mind," she interrupted hastily, blushing rosily as she shot a glance at Cole. Fortunately, he didn't seem to be paying a lot of attention to Jesse's comment. Instead, his eyes had gone a dark navy hue and he was again staring broodingly across the width of the room at Melanie. Sarah looked questioningly at Jesse, but he lifted a brow and shrugged his own confusion.

Sarah stared searchingly at Cole, looking for an answer for his unusual behavior. Women were always noticing Cole, flirting with him, and making passes at him. He never failed to meet their efforts with a lazy smile and a careless, easy masculine charm. She'd never seen him react like this. Although he lounged in his chair, his broad shoulders were tense under the white linen sportcoat and black shirt. Beneath his tawny hair, his handsome face with its high cheekbones and sculpted planes held a brooding quality. His thick lashes narrowed over eyes that darkened as he stared at the woman quietly listening to her companion, unaware of Cole's intent gaze.

Cole swung his gaze back to Sarah, caught her worried look, and forced his lips to curve upward in a semblance of a smile.

"So," he said, picking up their earlier conversation as if he'd never asked about Melanie, "have you picked out a name for this little girl?"

Clearly, Cole didn't want to be questioned, and Jesse and Sarah accepted his silent request. The three chatted with easy familiarity through the rest of dinner and dessert and were sipping coffee when the club's small dance band began a medley of mellow 1950's songs.

"Dance with me, honey," Jesse cajoled. "This is my kind of music."

Sarah laughed and he caught her hand to lead her through the tables and onto the dimly-lit, polished wood floor.

Cole watched the two with a half-smile as Sarah melted into Jesse's arms and they swayed slowly, rhythmically, until they disappeared amid the couples crowding the small dance floor. His gaze drifted over the other swaying couples and halted abruptly when it found a familiar splash of green silk and a fall of raven hair across bare shoulders.

Melanie was tired. If she hadn't promised Eric weeks ago that she would attend his faculty cocktail party, she would have begged off and gone to bed early with a good book. Later, she'd been too weary from smiling and making polite conversation to argue with him when he'd insisted on buying her dinner. Besides, the glass of white wine she'd nursed throughout the evening lay uneasily on her empty stomach, and she'd needed food to soak up the alcohol.

She always enjoyed the Lakeshore—its food, its atmosphere, and its small band—and she didn't object when Eric insisted she dance with him. One nice thing about Eric, she reflected as he moved her easily around the dance floor, was that he was so comfortable to be around. Like a brother. Or a well-worn shoe.

A smile curved her lips as she wondered how staid, predictable Eric would feel if he knew she was comparing him to a broken-in pair of loafers. Her gaze drifted idly across the dimly-lit restaurant and its occupants, moving slowly past a broad shouldered, tawny-haired man lounging casually in one of the dining chairs across the wide room, and on to the white-haired couple who occupied the next table before she froze, her slender form stiffening in Eric's arms. Her gaze snapped back to stare with startled, wide-eyed intensity.

It can't be him! she thought frantically. *He can't be here!*

But it was.

Cole McFadden was seated at the round table, twirling a stemmed wine glass slowly in his fingers, his enigmatic, deep blue eyes fastened narrowly on hers. She'd known he was in town, of course; the *CastleRock Independent* and the *Spirit Lake Beacon* had both run front-page articles about his racing accident and his return home to recuperate. But that had been almost two weeks ago. It hadn't occurred to her that he would still be around.

Time stood still while his gaze intently searched hers, and Melanie was terrified he would see through her shattered defenses to the hurt and pain walled deep within her. The band began the opening bars of a slow, dreamy love song, and, as if the music triggered a decision, Cole stood and began threading his way toward her, his unreadable blue gaze never leaving hers.

Melanie stiffened, her fingers clutching the shoulder of Eric's light-weave summer sports coat.

Surely he wouldn't—!

But he would. And he did.

The dance steps swung her away and turned her back on him, but, with unerring instinct, she knew he stood behind her before his finger tapped Eric's shoulder.

"Excuse me," he said, the low timbre of his voice stroking shivers up Melanie's spine. "May I cut in?"

Eric stopped dancing, his air of surprise quickly replaced by excited recognition.

"McFadden, isn't it? Aren't you the Cole McFadden who drives stock cars on the NASCAR circuit?"

Cole nodded in acknowledgment and looked down at Melanie's averted face.

"May I?"

"Oh, oh certainly. Of course!"

Eric beamed and relinquished her. It never occurred to him that Melanie might not want to dance with Cole, so he didn't ask her permission. Even if he had, she doubted that she could have spoken passed a throat gone dry with the desperate need to keep Cole from recognizing the emotion that welled and threatened to choke her.

Cole caught her cold fingers in his and rested his other hand on the curve of her waist where the soft green material, heated by the slim curves beneath it, was warm under his palm and fingertips.

Mechanically, Melanie lifted her left hand to his shoulder, staring blindly at her fingers lying against the white jacket. She could feel his gaze on her face, but she refused to lift her head and meet it. Not until she felt a little less shaky. Not until she felt she could speak without the tremors that quivered her insides affecting her voice.

Cole stared at her, trying to cope with the emotion that swamped him at the feel of her in his arms. The warm reality of holding her brought back a vivid memory of dancing with her on her father's lakeside dock. Then, his arms had been locked around her waist and hers around his neck, their bodies swaying in time to the music from her radio, lost in a world that consisted of only the two of them, body to body, mouth to mouth.

"Hello, Melanie," he said, his voice deeper, raspier than his usual bass.

She tilted her head back and looked up at him, her eyes shuttered and wary, a hint of vulnerability visible in the emerald depths.

"Hello, Cole," she answered, her own voice strained with the effort it took to keep it from shaking. "How are you?"

"Fine," he answered absently, "just fine." He indulged himself, letting his gaze run slowly over the delicate face turned up to his. "And you?"

"Fine," she repeated just as absently, "just fine." Her eyes were making their own tour of inspection. His sun-streaked blond hair was a shade shorter than it had been that summer eight years ago, but he still wore it side-parted and brushed back off his face. Fine lines etched pale rays at the corners of his eyes, the tan skin a bit more weathered where it smoothed over the hard bone structure of his face. He'd been youthfully handsome at twenty-five, but at thirty-three he was broader, heavier, with a mature masculinity that was more appealing. It made him more dangerous, she realized painfully. And more devastating, if she allowed him to find a chink in the frozen armor that had protected her battered, broken heart for eight long years. She searched for something to say to break the tense silence she suddenly realized had gone on far too long. "I read in the newspaper that you were injured during a race."

The broad shoulder beneath her hand lifted in a small shrug of dismissal.

"I did some damage to my leg."

Melanie pushed down the swift surge of sick dread that threatened her composure. He wasn't hers to worry over, and she couldn't afford to lose sight of the fact.

"Was anyone else hurt?" she managed to ask with polite interest.

"No, it was a one-car crash. I went into a wall and the car pretty much disintegrated. I was lucky to get out of it with only a broken leg." He felt a slight shudder tremble through the slim body so close to his. "Don't tell me you would have cared?" he said sardonically, tipping his head back to peer down into her averted face.

She lifted her eyes to his, quick anger flaring in the green depths.

"Of course, I would have cared! I hate to see anyone hurt!"

"Even me?" he said aloud with patent disbelief, his blue eyes holding self-mockery as they met hers.

"Of course, even you," she answered quickly, instinctively rejecting the inference that she didn't care.

Green eyes met blue for long moments and the sounds of the crowd around them faded away, leaving only the two of them snared by the knowledge of shared memories.

"Now why do I find that so hard to believe," he said softly, almost to himself.

"Maybe because you *wouldn't* have cared if the

positions were reversed,'' she said with a certain bitterness, and immediately regretted the words. But it was too late to recall them, and already his lashes were narrowing over eyes that gleamed with speculation.

''I can't imagine what would make you think that,'' he said.

''Really?'' Melanie's gaze dropped away from his and fastened unseeingly on her fingers resting against the white linen of his sportcoat. ''And I can't imagine why you would assume I would think anything else. Not after . . .''

''Not after . . . what?'' He prompted, his fingers tightening over hers, his arm going steel-hard against her waist. ''Not after you lied to me? Not after you let me believe you were a senior in college, when you were really a senior in high school? That you were only seventeen years old instead of the twenty-one I thought you were, and you'd been playing games that summer?'' His eyes sizzled with heat as they pinned hers, his voice rough with memory of the anger and betrayal he'd felt on that long-ago morning when he'd discovered her deception.

''Don't pretend you cared!'' she shot back at him, angry tears brimming and turning her eyes into shimmering emerald-green pools set in a black thicket of lashes. ''You left for the east coast and forgot about me—I received four letters from you! Four letters in two months!''

''I was working twenty-hour days! I was so damned exhausted that I fell into bed at night and dragged myself out three or four hours later, more dead than alive! And then I found out you weren't in college—you were still in high school. I was too damned old for you, and you were far too young to know if you wanted to commit your life to following a rookie driver from track to track. It wouldn't have been fair of me to ask it of you."

"I know that's the reason you gave me at the time," Melanie said, unconvinced as she remembered the sheer pain of reading that letter, "but I never believed my age was the real reason you wrote me that Dear John letter."

"Why not?" he said with frustration. "Maybe you didn't see the wisdom of my decision when you were seventeen, but surely now that you're older, you can see I was right. You were too young for the commitment I wanted from you."

Melanie's soft mouth curved in a small, faintly bitter smile. "My difficulty believing in your sincerity might have had something to do with the pictures of you and a series of beauty queens and rich women, and the articles in magazines and newspapers. You were obviously winning just as many contests off the track as on—what was it the columnists called you? The stud of the year?"

Cole winced, remembering those early days and the publicity that chronicled his every move.

"I'm not denying that I went to a few parties," he admitted. "Nor that some of the publicity wasn't justified. But most of it was just hype—gossip sells newspapers, whether it's truth or lies." The hand holding hers lifted to tilt her chin up so his gaze could search her green eyes. "I knew you were too young for me, and I knew I had to break it off. I dated other women and tried to forget you."

"Did it work?" she couldn't help asking, her voice husky. Her throat felt swollen, nearly closed with the effort to swallow tears.

"No," he said bluntly, his own voice rough with emotion. "No, it didn't work." His thumb brushed a tear from the curve of her cheek. "I came back at Christmas with some half-baked idea of working out a compromise, but your father wouldn't let me in the house. He was furious at me for dating his seventeen-year-old daughter, and I can't say I blame him."

Melanie gazed up at him, her mind going blank with shock. Could it be true? Had she misjudged him? Had her own frantic distress, coupled with the physical changes her body had been going through, clouded her ability to view the situation from a rational perspective? *No,* she told herself, rejecting the possibility. *It's just that he's so near—I never could think straight when his arms were around me. I'm not capable of being rational when he holds me.* She pulled her gaze from his with an effort and turned her face to rest her temple against his shoulder, the knubby weave of his sportcoat faintly rough and cool against her flushed cheek.

Cole's hand slid from her waist and up her back, his fingers spreading wide to caress silky skin. The thick fall of ebony hair swayed, brushing the satiny black strands against the back of his hand and his wrist where his cuff slid up, blanketing his hand above; while below, her bare skin was silky and warm beneath his palm. It evoked vivid memories of sultry summer nights, and that same silky hair brushing against his own naked skin. His lashes lowered, half-closing over blue eyes gone hot with need.

Cole let his eyes drift closed and his arms tightened, pulling her into the curve of his body until they were almost, but not quite, touching. She wore the same perfume now as she had during that long-ago summer and it drifted up to tease his nostrils. He bent his head, inhaling the mingled fragrance of perfume and warm woman which was uniquely Melanie.

Without speaking, they moved to the music, each caught up in their own memories of yesterday, each trying to match their dreams with the reality they touched. Hearts thudded faster, breath came more quickly out of lungs suddenly constricted within tightening chests.

Cole turned her, his thigh sliding against hers. Barely aware that she did so, Melanie shifted closer to him, obeying the unconsciously tightening circle of his arms and her own compulsive yearning to touch him. Her senses on overload, she realized dazedly that with no other human being had she ever felt this sense of rightness and of fitting together, like two halves of a puzzle to create a perfect whole.

Cole was having his own difficulties as he struggled to cope with the overwhelming feeling of homecoming that flooded him when her rigid body relaxed in his arms. He tightened his hold and eased her a fraction closer, until her body lay trustingly against his, their thighs brushing as they swayed to the music.

The contact sent a jolt of heat lightning through Melanie's veins that shocked her back to awareness, and she stiffened and shifted away from him. Her physical response was just as powerful as if they'd been lovers only yesterday. She couldn't rely on her mind's ability to control her body's headlong tumble into desire at his touch. And she knew she had to drive a wedge between them to restore the distance that had kept them out of each other's orbit for so long.

"I'm glad we had this talk," she said gravely, forcing her gaze to meet his. "If we chance to meet on the street now, I won't feel uncomfortable about saying hello." As she spoke, the song ended and the band announced that it was taking a ten-minute break. She dropped her hand from his shoulder and stepped back, tugging her fingers from his grasp. "I hope you enjoy your stay in CastleRock and that your leg mends so you can return to racing soon. Good-bye." Her words were stiffly polite. She held out her hand, and he took it in his. But instead of providing a barrier between them, the gesture only produced a warm point of contact between their bodies.

"Not good-bye, Melanie."

His unreadable gaze searched hers for a long moment until, silently, she tore her eyes from his, turned her back, and walked off the small dance floor, painfully aware of the warm weight of his hand lying possessively against her waist as he accompanied her. She refused to meet his gaze as he seated her, murmured his thanks, and left.

"I didn't know you knew Cole McFadden, Melanie!" Eric's brown eyes gleamed with enthusiasm behind his wire-frame glasses. "Did you go to school with him?"

"No," Melanie shook her head, struggling to keep her features from revealing the storm of emotions that raged inside her. "No, I went to a girls' school in Allentown. I didn't go to public school in CastleRock."

"Then how did you meet him?"

"Oh, the usual way," Melanie managed to get out. "CastleRock is a small town, I suppose we just sort of saw each other around. You know how it is."

Eric stared at her, a perplexed frown on his face.

Before he could ask any more questions, Melanie hurried into speech.

"Do you suppose we could make an early night of it, Eric? I have the most frightful headache."

He would have pursued his questioning, but one look at her pale face was enough to arouse his sympathy. Melanie collected her purse, and they left the club. She scrupulously avoided glancing across the room where she knew Cole sat, although she felt his brooding gaze like a hot weight against her back.

TWO

Melanie couldn't sleep. The headache she'd pretended to have had become a nagging reality before Eric walked her to her door, and the aspirin she took failed to cure it. By three a.m., the sheets on her bed were tangled from her restless tossing and turning.

It's no use, she finally acknowledged wearily as she slid from the four-poster brass bed and crossed to the window. *I'm not going to be able to sleep tonight.*

The moonlight winked its way past the wire mesh of the screen and into her bedroom, and brushed her still figure with cool, pale light, making deep, mysterious pools of her green eyes beneath the delicate arch of black brows, and turning her long black hair into a cape of silvered ebony. It stroked across her arms and throat, left bare by the brief white satin camisole and tap pants she wore.

I don't want to remember, she told the silent, sympathetic moon with stubborn anguish. *I won't—it does no good!*

But it seemed she had no choice. Seeing Cole after all this time, and feeling his arms around her, had wedged open the locked door in her heart behind which she had sealed all her memories of that brief, happy summer when she was seventeen—and its tragic ending. Now, those memories were clamoring to be heard, demanding to be let out, and despite her determined, nearly frantic refusals over the last several hours, she was losing the battle. Melanie was too tired to fight any longer. She gave in, the view outside her window slipping out of focus as her thoughts turned inward, seeing once again the naive and innocent young girl she had been eight years ago.

The hot July night was quiet, the boards of the old dock Melanie sat on smooth and water-worn beneath her fingertips. She perched on the end of the T-shaped dock, her bare feet and tanned legs dangling over the edge and swinging idly as she stared out across the lake. A full moon rode high overhead, its clear light casting a path of gold across the smooth surface of the water.

It was barely ten o'clock, but already the lights were winking off in the houses on either side of her along the lakeshore. The Winters' immediate neighbors were all either older retired people or middle-aged couples with married children. None of them had teenagers Melanie's age, and, as a result, summers spent in CastleRock were periods of lonely isolation for her.

Unconsciously releasing a heavy sigh, she stared at the fat yellow moon. Maybe this summer she could convince her parents to let her attend CastleRock's West High School in the fall, instead of going back to St. Catherine's School for Girls in Allentown. After all, it would be her senior year, and her last chance to go to public high school before graduation.

The roar of a speedboat motor interrupted her thoughts and she glanced to her right. The running lights of a ski boat were approaching fast, the wake it raised as it cut through the water sending miniature waves to slap softly against the dock as it passed. The laughter of the boat's occupants carried easily across the water and intensified Melanie's sense of lonely isolation as the boatload of young people sped away, following the curve of the shoreline.

The boat's running lights grew smaller and nearly disappeared against the lights on the ends of docks and the houselights on shore. Melanie stared after the boat, wishing she were a part of the laughing group, when she realized the lights were no longer fading, but were once again growing brighter.

The boat had circled and was retracing its path along the shoreline. It slowed as it neared Melanie, nearly stopping some two hundred yards offshore. Melanie watched with curiosity as one of the people in the boat stood. Illuminated by the moon, the man was a tall, broad figure without features who stripped a shirt off over his head, and with one smooth movement dove over thc edge of the boat and into the water.

"Hey, Cole! Come back here!" a laughing malc voice called.

"Come back, Cole! I promise I'll take you back to the dock," called a feminine voice.

The man paused, treading water while he faced the boat.

"Sure you will, Carol," the deep voice was wryly disbelieving, "you told me that an hour ago!"

"This time I promise I will," the girl answered, the clear tones underlaid with husky invitation. "Please, get back in the boat."

"Nope," the swimmer turned his back on the boat. "I'm going home. Y'all be careful now," he drawled over his shoulder, and then he swam toward shore, his powerful arms pulling him through the water with ease.

Behind him, the remaining five occupants of the boat called after him, but he ignored their cajoling, teasing, and coaxing, and after a few moments they gave up. The boat's engine revved and with a spray of water accelerated away across the lake.

Melanie watched with fascinated anticipation as the swimmer drew closer and she realized he was heading directly for the dock where she sat. Her fingers gripped the worn wood, her feet ceasing their slow movements in the water as she waited for him to notice her.

But he didn't. Not until he was a short six feet from the dock's edge. Then his head lifted and he stopped swimming abruptly, treading water while he stared at her.

Cole knew he was close to the edge of the dock and paused to gauge just how close. But it wasn't just the dock edge he saw when he looked up to get his bearings. Seated on the end of the wooden structure he was aiming for was a girl, silently watching him. Startled, his quick, assessing glance registered slim, shapely legs dangling over the edge of the dock, a slender curved body in white shorts and a halter top, and an intriguing face sculptured with moonlight and shadows beneath a long fall of dark hair tucked behind her left ear and spilling forward in a long sheaf over her right shoulder.

"Hi," he said, realizing that he'd been silently staring at her.

"Hi," she answered, her voice softly shy.

The husky tones sent rivulets of arousal curling in his midsection, and Cole's eyes narrowed over her still figure.

"Mind if I use your dock?" he asked.

"Not at all," Melanie answered, a shiver of anticipation teasing its way up her spine.

Water ran in streams off powerful flexed muscles when he placed the flat of his palms on the surface of the dock and pulled himself easily out of the water and twisted to sit beside her. Fascinated, Melanie openly stared at him. His hair gleamed darkly gold under the moonlight and was sleeked back from his forehead, exposing the hard angles of high cheekbones and a firm jaw. Beneath the dark arch of his brows, his eyes returned her stare just as frankly.

Heat flushed her cheeks and she dropped her lashes briefly, but she couldn't pull her gaze away from him. Faded, cut-off jeans, so short the ends of the white pockets peeked from beneath the ragged edges, rode low on his hips, and heavily muscled thighs were traced with silky, dark gold hair. His chest was smooth and sleek, muscles sharply defining his pectorals and making a washboard of hard ridges across his midriff.

Like her, he curled his fingers over the edge of the dock's worn boards and leaned slightly forward, the muscles in his upper arms and forearms flexing and rippling beneath sleek skin as he moved. Melanie drew a deep breath into starved lungs and was instantly aware of spicy male aftershave, of coconut-based tanning lotion on skin warmed by a day spent in the sun, and of the underlying, distinctive scent of cool lakewater.

Cole felt her curious gaze moving over his wet body as if her eyes were soft hands, stroking him. His body reacted with instant heat and he wondered with bemusement if he was turning the lakewater that dripped from him into steam. Suddenly aware that he was sitting silently, staring at her as if he were mute, he forced his throat muscles to work.

"My name's Cole," he got out. "Cole McFadden."

"I'm Melanie," she answered, her voice husky with the effort it took to focus on his words and form a response.

"Melanie," he repeated, lingering caressingly over the word. "Pretty name."

Melanie's cheeks burned with hot color. "Thank you," she murmured. "My mother fell in love with it when she read *Gone With The Wind.*"

A bare six inches separated their bodies, but neither questioned their inability to remember the normal, polite responses required by society's rules. His gaze moved slowly, intently, over her face, but she couldn't tell what color his eyes were and she wanted, needed to know.

"What color are your eyes?" she asked, her gaze fastened on his.

"Blue," he said softly, trying to determine the exact shade of her own thick-lashed eyes and failing. "What color are yours?"

"Green," she responded with the same hushed tones.

"Dark green or light green?"

"Just plain old green."

"No," he answered softly, positively, "there's not a thing about you that's plain—they must be green as new spring grass, or green as emeralds, or the deep green of the lake after the spring thaw."

She laughed, a husky chuckle of delight, her mouth curving upward into a smile that drew an answering grin from Cole.

"No," she shook her head, sending her hair shifting down her back, "just plain old green."

"I don't believe it," he said. The hand gripping the dock only a scant few inches from her bare knee lifted to slide gently, testingly through the thick fall of her silky hair. "And I don't believe your hair is 'just dark,' either."

"No, it's black," Melanie said breathlessly, his hand in her hair stealing the breath from her lungs. "Just black."

"Hmmm," he grinned, his teeth flashing whitely against dark skin. "Black as night? Ebony? Raven black?"

"No, just plain black," she smiled back at him, entranced by his smile and snared by the web of sensual awareness that spun between them.

Cole froze, caught by the same awareness that held Melanie. A cloud drifted across the face of the moon and the resulting deepening of the night around them pulsed and throbbed in the heated silence.

"Melanie . . ." Cole breathed, his fingers tightening in the thick silk of her hair.

Her breath caught, her gaze fastening on his mouth as his head slowly lowered toward hers and her body swayed unconsciously to meet his.

"Melanie! Melanie, are you down there?"

Her mother's voice broke the taut silence. Melanie's eyes snapped open and with dismay, she saw Cole freeze into stillness, his face only inches from hers.

"Melanie—your father wants you to help him program the VCR. Melanie?"

"I have to go," Melanie whispered, knowing that if she didn't respond, her mother would leave the deck and follow the path across the lawn and down the slope to the dock. For some indefinable reason, she didn't want to share the magic that wrapped her and Cole together. Never before had she felt this instant communication with another human, this feeling that he knew all her secrets and understood each one.

"Can I see you tomorrow?" he asked, unable to let her go without a promise of another meeting.

"Yes—oh, yes," she breathed, unable to be coy. "Call me—my number is 285–4121. Will you remember? I don't have anything to write it on."

"I'll remember," he said with a quiet conviction that reassured her.

His fingers slipped reluctantly from her hair and they stood, his broad, muscled body looming over her slender shape.

"Don't forget," Melanie implored with sudden intensity, her fingers reaching to rest against the bare, hard muscles of his chest.

Cole's hand swiftly covered hers, pressing the soft palm and fingers against his warm skin.

"I won't forget," he promised with the same deep intensity. And with a suddenness that took them both by surprise, he dropped his head and brushed the soft lushness of her mouth with his. The contact was brief but it sent a jolt of heat lightning through them both.

Surprised and too inexperienced to hide her reaction, Melanie gasped, her hand turning in his to clutch his fingers. "Cole. . . ?" she whispered, her green eyes searching his.

Cole returned the clinging grip and would have lowered his mouth to hers, but once again the woman's voice intruded.

"Melanie—where are you?"

"I have to go." Reluctantly, she tugged her fingers from his and ran lightly down the length of the dock. She reached the bottom of the steps leading up the bank to the lawn and turned to look back. His features were indistinct in the shadowed moonlight as she lifted a hand to wave before she swiftly climbed the shallow steps and disappeared.

She was crying. Melanie lifted shaking fingertips to wipe the warm wetness from her cheeks, tasting the salty flavor of tears at the corners of her mouth.

"Damn you, Cole," she whispered out loud, as tears continued to leak from her eyes, echoing the crying pain of her heart. Even after eight years, memories of how much she had loved him and the depth of his betrayal brought a surge of fresh grief that defied her father's assurances that time healed all wounds. The wounds inflicted by her one venture into love weren't healed. Deep inside her, the pain was as fresh as if Cole had left her only yesterday.

Across town, in the big old Victorian house owned by Jeannie and Gavin McFadden, Cole lay awake, staring at the ceiling of the room he'd shared with his brother, Trace, until he'd left home. Tonight he had the room to himself, for Trace had long since bought his own house and sixteen months ago had married.

The same demons that had haunted him for the last eight years tortured him. The same unanswered questions still defied explanation. He remembered every moment with Melanie, beginning with the second he dove out of the boat into the lake, stopped swimming, and looked up to see her watching him from the end of her parents' dock.

He'd turned twenty-five that summer and been single-mindedly, fiercely career-oriented. He'd worked his way steadily upward on the NASCAR circuit since graduation from West High School seven years before. When he signed a contract a week earlier with a major stock car racing sponsor, he exulted with the knowledge that he was on the verge of success. Due to sponsor conflicts, he found himself with an unexpected holiday, and returned to CastleRock to spend the months of July and August with his family before reporting to his new race team.

Falling in love was the farthest thing from his mind, but from the moment he pulled himself out of the lake and onto Melanie's dock, he'd been intrigued and fascinated by the beautiful brunette. They'd spent every moment possible together, and he'd been so besotted with her that it didn't occur to him to wonder why she never introduced him to her parents or friends. He thought she felt the same unwillingness as he did to share their time with others, so he never questioned her. Nor did he guess how young she was. She had a mature dignity underlaid with an innocence that delighted him. When he assumed that she was in college, she didn't deny it, although she never actually lied to him.

Head over heels in love, he'd asked her to marry him and had reluctantly agreed when she insisted she had to finish school first. He'd tried to convince her to transfer to a college on the east coast so that they could be together, but she refused. So, on September first, he left for South Carolina and she left CastleRock to return to school. They'd both promised to write, and he'd promised to see her at Thanksgiving. Melanie had been a far better correspondent than he, for his new schedule was gruelling, but he thought of her constantly, dreamed of her nightly, and missed her so much the ache became a constant companion. Then, during the first week of November, his mother sent him a long, newsy letter and enclosed a copy of the local CastleRock newspaper. Usually, Cole read the paper from cover to cover, but this time, the picture on page three and the caption below stopped him. He easily recognized Melanie in the grainy black-and-white picture, and didn't need confirmation in the printed line below to see the family resemblance in the older man and woman with her. The picture had been taken at an award ceremony honoring her father and his bank, but the brief blurb accompanying the photo identified Melanie as their daughter, a senior at St. Catherine's High School for Girls in Allentown. Stunned, Cole called his mother. She knew the Winters and confirmed their daughter's age. Angry and heart sore, Cole had done the only thing possible under the circumstances. He wrote Melanie and broke off their relationship, telling her that he was too old for her and she too young for him. She didn't write back.

The ceiling Cole stared at slowly faded out of focus and his gaze turned inward, remembering how he'd held out and clung to good intentions until Christmas. Unable to forget her or to live with the empty hole where his heart once beat, he risked breaking his contract and flew home to Iowa to see her.

It was snowing. Not with the serious, wind-driven flakes that heralded a blizzard, but with big, soft flakes that drifted lazily earthward as if their sole purpose was to gently blanket an already white-covered earth. It was a good fifty degrees colder in Iowa than in the comparatively warm Georgia December he'd left behind at the airport that morning, and Cole hunched his shoulders beneath the worn high school letter jacket of blue wool and cream leather. He climbed out of the car he'd borrowed from his brother Trace and hesitated by the front fender of the orange Camaro, shoving his hands deep into his jacket pockets as he stared at the imposing, two-story lakeshore home. Lights glowed from the downstairs windows and through the curtains of a second floor glass pane.

Nerves tightened and quivered in his gut, but he squared his shoulders and moved up the shovelled walk between the piled-up snow that lined the concrete squares. *If she won't see me,* he told himself philosophically, *then she won't see me. Nothing ventured, nothing gained.* But even as he thought the words, he knew he lied. If she refused to speak to him, he wasn't sure his heart would survive.

He climbed the clean-swept steps to the porch and stretched out a forefinger to push the doorbell, then returned his hands to his jacket pockets while the bell echoed inside the house. Only moments later the porchlight flicked on overhead and the heavy inner door swung open. The stocky man in shirtsleeves who held the edge of the door, a newspaper in one hand and reading glasses perched on the bridge of his nose, bore a startling resemblance to Melanie, with his black hair—brushed at the temples with silver—and the deep emerald green of his eyes beneath black brows.

"Good evening," John Winters said pleasantly, his green eyes reflecting only mild curiosity as they swept over the clean-cut young man standing on his front porch.

"Good evening," Cole responded automatically. "Is Melanie home?"

"Yes, she is, but . . ." Melanie's father paused in mid-sentence, green eyes narrowing as he swiftly reassessed Cole's broad-shouldered figure. Suspicion darkened his eyes and a frown creased his features. "Who are you?" he demanded bluntly.

"Cole McFadden—I'm a friend of Melanie's, sir, and I'd like to see her if . . ."

"No!" As Cole spoke, John Winters' figure stiffened, the frown growing into a black glare. "Absolutely not! Even if she wanted to, *which she doesn't,* I wouldn't let her!"

Nonplussed, Cole stared at the irate man. He'd half-expected some difficulty in getting Melanie to talk to him, but the enraged response from her father left him bewildered.

"But, Mr. Winters, all I want to do is talk to her . . ."

"I wouldn't let you within a mile of my daughter! You're too damned old for her—eight years too old!

She's only seventeen and far too young and innocent, and she damned sure didn't deserve what you did to her! Now get off my porch and off my land, before I give in to the temptation to run you off with a shotgun for what you did to my little girl!"

Stunned, Cole found himself facing a closed door, slammed with a resounding crash. He stared blankly at the solid symbol of the barrier that lay between him and Melanie before he turned and moved slowly across the porch, down the steps, and along the snow-dusted walkway to his car. Oblivious to the cold and the snowflakes clinging to his bare head and upturned collar, he paused at his car, staring unseeingly at the white flakes that melted as soon as they landed on the engine-warmed hood. He turned to look back at the house, his gaze moving from the closed door to the second-floor window. A slender shape was highlighted by the lamplight and his heart leapt as he realized the silhouette belonged to Melanie. For a long moment, he stared upward. But then she slowly pulled the shade down, closing him away from her sight, shutting him out of her life.

Even now, the memory of the pain and the awful finality in her gesture turned a knife inside him, and Cole grimaced, shifting restlessly against the sheets.

He'd returned to the racing circuit after spending Christmas Day with his family, and he'd sworn to forget her, believing that she was only playing summer games while he'd fallen in love—hard, fast, and forever.

He'd never forgotten her, and he'd never gotten answers for the questions that still plagued him. Why did she refuse to see him that Christmas? Had she been too young for the commitment he'd wanted? Had he somehow talked her into agreeing to a marriage she didn't want? Could it have been that she was too young at seventeen to fight her father's anger?

He stacked his hands beneath his head and stared unblinkingly at the dark ceiling.

If Melanie was too young to be involved with me at seventeen, she damned sure isn't now, he thought, thick lashes narrowing over his eyes. He couldn't have misread the awareness that trembled through her body when it brushed against his earlier as they danced at the Lakeshore. Whatever she had felt at seventeen, whether it was just old-fashioned lust or something more, was still there at twenty-five. The intervening eight years hadn't changed the way their bodies reacted to each other. Melanie Winters was an unfinished chapter in his life that he refused to leave unended any longer.

Whatever the results, he decided, as dawn shaded the eastern sky with mauve and pink and the room lightened from blackness to grey shadows, he would roll the dice once more. He'd either wipe out this grinding need that wouldn't leave him alone, or he'd find again the love that had once turned his world to golden sunshine and simmering summer heat.

The shop was blessedly quiet. It wasn't that Melanie wanted customers to stay away, but she couldn't help but feel thankful that business was slow. Her alarm had awakened her at seven a.m., as usual, but although the headache that had plagued her the night before was gone, her mirror reflected lavender shadows below eyes that were heavy-lidded from the flood of tears she'd shed. Carefully applied makeup covered much of the outward signs, but nothing could erase the emotion that lurked just below the surface.

Determinedly forcing thoughts of Cole from her mind, Melanie concentrated on removing a floral bra and panties from a mannequin atop a glass display counter at the back of the shop. She slipped a red silk and lace teddy over the armless, legless mannequin, and was adjusting the narrow straps over the plaster shoulders when the bell over the shop door jingled merrily.

She forced a welcoming smile to her lips and glanced over her shoulder, but her fingers froze over the slender strips of red silk when Cole's broad-shouldered figure stepped over the threshold.

"Good morning," Cole smiled, but he winced inwardly as the welcoming curve of Melanie's lips faded. He pushed the door shut behind him, the bell jingling.

"Good morning," Melanie managed to get out. To her vast relief, her voice didn't tremble.

He wanted to walk straight across the polished hardwood floor that separated them and take her in his arms. She was wearing a white sheath, its simple lines faithfully following the curves of her body from shoulder to mid-knee. A double row of black buttons the size of half dollars marched from the modest low curve of the neckline to mid-thigh. Her hair was a long fall of black silk, and the crisp white of the dress accented the golden tanned skin beneath the short, tailored cap sleeves and hem.

Somehow he managed to restrain himself, and with an effort he ripped his gaze away from her and glanced casually around the shop. Wedding gowns lined the wall to the right of the door, and to his left round chrome racks held hangers draped with lacy lingerie. The floor was polished oak, with Oriental rugs scattered across the gleaming surface, and the furnishings were antiques. An 1800s' bureau in golden oak stood against one wall, blue and white lingerie spilling from its open drawers in an artistic display.

"This is really nice," he said, his voice unconsciously reflecting an honest pride in her accomplishment.

"Thank you." Melanie glanced around the shop, pulling her gaze away from him. A blue cotton, button-up shirt covered his broad shoulders and chest, and faded Levis smoothed over the powerful muscles of his thighs. The sun had bleached his blond hair in streaks. Combined with his deep tan, it made his eyes a startling, Caribbean-sea blue. "I like it."

"It shows—it looks like you."

"It looks like me?" Her face reflected her confusion, a little vee pulling down the arch of black brows. "What do you mean?"

"The antiques—the way it's put together." Blue eyes flicked over the mauve-and-blue rugs and the blend of colorful fabrics in their displays. "The colors and the quality of the merchandise." His mouth quirked in a grin as his blue gaze moved on to fasten with absorbed concentration on her face. "It has class."

Melanie felt the heat move up her throat and into her cheeks, but managed to return his gaze with a level look.

"That's kind of you—I've put a lot of time and energy into Victoria's Garden." Her voice held a quiet pride.

"It shows." Cole tore his eyes away from their fascinated absorption with the contrast of thick-lashed green eyes against smooth tanned skin and the lush pink of her mouth, and glanced around the shop once more. Shoving his hands into his back pockets, he strolled across the oak floor toward her, pausing in front of an oval standing mirror. He reached out to finger a fragile white nightgown draped over the mirror's oak frame, the lace of the gown creating a fine, transparent cobweb against the dark skin of his hand. An instant image of the delicate white gown covering Melanie's bare body imprinted itself on his brain.

Melanie tried to ignore the curl of reaction in her midsection at the sight of his dark, very male hand against the feminine silk and lace, but then his gaze lifted slowly to meet hers and she was trapped by the heated flare of arousal in the blue depths. Awareness arched between them with white hot light, sucking the air from her lungs and sending her heart shuddering in reaction. For a long, relentless moment he held her gaze and she couldn't move, couldn't breathe. Then he blinked, slowly releasing her. Heart pounding, she abruptly turned her back to him.

"Were you shopping for anything in particular?" The faint tremble in her voice matched the quiver in her fingers as she concentrated intently on slipping the fabric loops over the teddy's tiny, red satin-covered buttons. "If you don't see what you want, I can always order it." Determinedly, she refused to acknowledge an inward twist of pain at the thought of Cole buying lingerie for another woman.

Cole eyed her slim back and his fingers fell away from the white silk.

"Actually, I only stopped to see you," he said, walking closer to lean casually against the counter beside her. "I thought we could have lunch together."

Startled, Melanie stiffened, her fingers stilling their movements against the red silk as her head turned slowly, her hair sliding silkily forward over one shoulder as her gaze met his.

"I don't think that's a good idea," she said, her thick lashes falling to half-conceal her eyes after that one startled moment. She turned back to the mannequin.

"Why not? Don't you eat lunch?" he asked.

"Not always."

"Not always," he repeated slowly. "How about today? Are you planning to eat lunch today?"

"Actually, I was," she replied coolly, glancing sideways at him.

"Then why can't we eat together?" he said persuasively.

"I don't think it's a good idea," she answered.

"And there's no reason for us to have lunch together."

"People don't need a reason to share a lunch table," he said. "But if you need a reason, we're old friends. We can talk over old times."

Her slim form stiffened. Her fingers stilled and stopped toying with the red silk, and shoulders squared, she turned to face him.

"We're not old friends," she said with cool calm, her green gaze meeting his with direct force. "We're used-to-be lovers. It's been a long time since we were teenagers and we're older, different people now. There's nothing left of the boy and girl we used to be, and we have nothing in common anymore."

Cole stared at her, his blue eyes narrowing assessingly over her features. Her voice held cool rejection, but beneath her composed assurance lay a vulnerability that belied her firm words, and her hands were curled into tight fists at her sides.

"*You* were a teenager," he said evenly. "I was twenty-five and a man. I'm older now and so are you, but we're not all that different. And the way you felt in my arms last night told me that we still strike sparks off each other."

"No, that's not true—you're wrong," Melanie refused to acknowledge the twinge her conscience made at the lie. "There isn't anything between us but a few old memories."

"Are you telling me you didn't feel anything when we danced together last night?"

"That's exactly what I'm telling you." The green eyes that met Cole's held a stubborn defiance.

He didn't believe her. Her lips told him one thing, her body another. Her slim form was strung taut with tension, and the soft curve of her mouth trembled faintly.

"I don't believe you," he said softly. "Prove it."

Startled, Melanie's green eyes reflected brief confusion before a veil dropped to conceal her emotions.

"Don't be ridiculous," she said with commendable calm. "You'll just have to accept my word that there's no attraction between us—there isn't any way to prove I'm not attracted to you."

"Sure there is." And with a swiftness that left her no time to protest, Cole stepped closer and slid his arms around her waist. His mouth found hers with unerring precision.

THREE

"Mmmph," Melanie tried to protest, but his lips muffled her words. She stepped backward to elude him, but was halted abruptly by the waist-high counter. He followed her, his body warm and solid against hers as he trapped her within the circle of his arms, her retreat defeated by the counter behind her and Cole in front of her.

Cole knew she wasn't cooperating, but that didn't stop him. Her slim form was stiff with stunned surprise, her mouth firmly closed beneath his, but that didn't alter the fact that this was Melanie he held in his arms. He'd waited eight long years for this moment, and he'd nearly given up hoping it would ever happen.

His mouth moved with slow persuasion over hers, one big hand gently cradling the back of her head.

Melanie's protests grew weaker until they ceased completely, her lips trembling and warm beneath his. Her hands stopped pushing at his chest, and instead they closed into tight fists, gripping handfuls of his shirt for support as her body went suddenly boneless against his. She thought she'd made herself forget how big, hard-muscled, and warm his body was; how small, safe, and protected she'd always felt in his arms; and how his mouth had seduced her when it moved with warm enticement against hers.

Dear God! She thought with panic. *I didn't forget, I just refused to remember!* It was her last coherent thought before she gave in to the irresistible wave of sensation that swamped her.

Cole felt her surrender to the raging inferno that roared out of control between them, and he gathered her closer, molding her slender, curved body to his much larger frame, groaning against her mouth as she allowed it without protest. Their bodies pressed together, from mouths to knees, with an overwhelming sense of homecoming and rightness. For long moments he forgot that they stood in a public shop.

A car backfiring in the street outside the cool interior of Victoria's Garden penetrated Cole's absorption and jolted him back to earth. His arms tightened like steel bands, protesting his mind's command to let her go before someone walked in and saw them. He didn't give a damn for himself, but he didn't want to embarrass Melanie. Reluctantly, he lifted his mouth from hers and looked down at her.

"Melanie?" He watched as her heavy lashes lifted to reveal green eyes dazed and drowsy with emotion.

Melanie stared up at him, unable to force her stunned senses to respond. Her heart shuddered, thundering and pounding in her ears and slamming against her ribcage, and she tried to speak but her vocal chords refused to function.

"If this isn't *attraction,* honey," he growled softly, his breath puffing warmly against her damp lips, "then it's damn sure the closest thing there is to it, and it'll do until the real thing comes along."

Melanie blinked, her thick, sooty lashes dropping slowly to conceal her emerald eyes before lifting again.

Cole watched her struggle to absorb his words and form an answer. With a surge of fierce satisfaction, he realized that she was just as affected by their kiss as he was.

"I . . . ," she managed to get out, her voice only a husky murmur. But her traitorous body still rested against his, sending mind-numbing signals to a brain that struggled to remember this was the one man she couldn't have. It didn't matter that he was the one man she wanted. She tried speaking again, and this time managed to form words. "I'm not willing to settle for anything less than the real thing. I don't want to have an affair with you, Cole."

Cole heard the determination beneath her husky whisper. With an effort, he forced his arms to leave her and he would have stepped back and away from her, but her fingers were tangled in the blue cotton of his shirt front. His calloused fingers closed over hers and gently uncurled them, trapping her slender hands in his when she tried to pull free.

"Okay, Melanie, you don't want an affair," he repeated, his own voice gravelly. "But I still want to see you."

"No, Cole," Melanie forced her lips to say the words and felt them tear a giant jagged hole in her heart. "I don't think it would be wise, or safe."

"Safe? Wise?" His deep voice echoed hers. "I don't think those are words I understand." When she started to voice an objection, he merely shook his head in frustration. This was neither the time nor the place to convince her that she was wrong. Any moment, a customer might walk through the shop's door and interrupt them. He needed to find a way to get her alone, away from distractions and interruptions, and if she wouldn't agree to normal dates, then he'd just have to think of something else.

He gently opened her hands and dropped a soft kiss against each one. The feel of his warm lips moving in a soft caress against the sensitive skin of her palms stole her breath. Her heart ached and tears threatened as she looked down at the crown of his head and the short mane of thick blond hair that covered it. How well she remembered threading her fingers through its soft thickness while his mouth plundered hers. Before her tears spilled, he'd reluctantly released her and was striding away from her across the oak flooring to the outer door.

"I'm leaving, but I'm not giving up," he said softly, his words holding a promise. "I'll just have to find a way to convince you that I'm not so dangerous."

Melanie watched the door close on his broad back, the bell jingling in the suddenly quiet shop.

Not dangerous? She thought incredulously. He had no idea how dangerous he was to her peace of mind! She was furious with herself for having failed to foresee this encounter. Cole had never been a man to give up easily and even though he'd left, she knew she hadn't seen the last of him. She had no doubt that he had an alternate plan and the knowledge made her uneasy. She should have known when she looked up into his darkened eyes after their dance at the Lakeshore that he wanted her.

Oh, yes, she admitted with painful honesty, she'd recognized that look. What she'd failed to take into account, she realized, was her own desire. She wanted, too. She needed, with a force that had stunned her. After all this time, after all the lessons she thought she'd learned from Cole McFadden, still she'd ached for his hands on her, craved the taste and texture of his mouth against hers, and her body had melted to flow like warm honey against his.

It's just chemistry, she told herself stubbornly. *We were always physically compatible. Incredibly so.* For a moment, she considered the possibility that maybe she'd turned to fire and smoke in his arms because the love she'd once felt for him hadn't been destroyed and erased by the years. Perhaps, instead, it had lain dormant, growing only stronger from its forced suppression.

No, she pushed the thought from her mind, but it stubbornly refused to be confined and instead, bounced back to the surface. *No, I don't still love him, and even if my body wants his, I won't give in. I refuse to be that stupid and irresponsible again, not when I know the price I've already paid once. Never again!* Her fingers unconsciously smoothed over the flat concave curve of her belly in an instinctively protective gesture. She stared unseeingly at the warm oak wood of the floor where sunlight spilled a pool of gold, ambushed by memories that catapulted her back to the icy cold of that long-ago November.

Oh, no! Melanie stared with agonized eyes at the home pregnancy kit. *Positive? It can't be positive. I can't be pregnant! I can't!*

The bell for morning classes had rung a half hour before, and the halls and rooms of St. Catherine's dormitory had emptied with their usual miraculous speed. Melanie, fighting down the nausea she'd struggled with for the last two weeks, had reported in sick to the floor monitor and waited until her roommate left for class before smuggling the pregnancy test kit to the communal bathroom. Nibbling nervously on a fingernail, she'd followed the instructions printed on the box and waited with dread for the results.

Now she had them. And she wished she didn't.

She hugged her arms tightly over her roiling stomach and stared at her reflection in the long mirror that stretched over the line of sinks against one wall. Dark circles etched the fragile skin beneath green eyes that were filled with despair, and her black hair lay in a dishevelled braid over one shoulder against the blue-sprigged flannel of her nightgown.

She wanted Cole, her heart cried. She needed

Cole, to hold her, to tell her everything would be all right, to tell her that he wanted her and the child they had created. But Cole didn't want her. And he'd made it perfectly clear in the letter he'd written in late October that he was furious with her for not telling him she was still in high school and letting him believe she was a senior in college. He'd said that she was too young for him, and that he was far too old for her.

Tears welled, spilling over her lashes to leave damp tracks down her pale cheeks, seeping their warm, salty wetness onto lips gone dry with heartbreak and hopelessness.

How can I tell Mom and Daddy? The mere thought made her feel even more ill, and her stomach heaved in protest, sending her racing for the nearest commode.

As it turned out, nature took care of telling her parents. She returned to her parents' home in CastleRock for Christmas vacation, dreading the revelation that she knew would shatter their faith in her. But the first night she was home, before she could steel herself to tell them, violent cramps and bleeding woke her from her sleep. Her terrified parents raced her to the emergency room and stood by helplessly while the hospital staff tried to prevent a miscarriage. Melanie didn't realize how much she wanted the baby until it was snatched from her, and her parents didn't need to ask who the father was, for she cried out for Cole when she was nearly unconscious with the pain.

The bell on the shop door jingled and Melanie

blinked slowly and forced a smile for the three chattering teen-agers who entered.

No, she told herself with bleak conviction. *I'll never be that stupid again. The price is too high.*

The cavernous interior of McFadden's Classic Cars was dim and cool. Cole perched on a high wooden stool, his long legs clad in faded, grease-stained Levis, a ripped T-shirt with a *McFadden Racing Team* logo across the front covering his chest. His battered tennis shoes were propped on the rungs of the stool and drops of cool moisture beaded the can of soda that dangled from the fingers of one hand.

". . . you ought to come tonight, Cole." Kelly Matthews, the collar of his paramedic uniform unbuttoned and tie askew, leaned against the fender of a 1938 Ford coupe.

Kelly's voice saying his name yanked Cole's thoughts away from the problem of how to get Melanie alone. He'd viewed the difficulty from all angles for three days, but so far hadn't arrived at a solution.

"Sorry, Kelly—what did you say? I should go where?"

Kelly lifted an eyebrow at Trace, but Cole's brother only grinned and shrugged his shoulders before returning his attention to the stubborn bolt on the Ford's engine.

"I said you ought to get out and circulate—the Women's Club is having it's annual fund-raiser tonight, you should come with me."

"Nah," Cole grunted, taking a swig of his soda. "Fund-raisers aren't my idea of a good time."

"Usually they're not mine either, but this year they're auctioning off bachelors. And one of them is me."

"What?" Cole stared at Kelly as if the younger man had lost his mind.

"You heard me—the single women of CastleRock are going to bid on twelve bachelors. Each of us planned a weekend and the highest bidder gets us for two fun-filled days. And nights, if we're lucky," Kelly added, leering suggestively.

"Hah," Trace hooted from under the hood. "In your dreams, Matthews!"

"Well, you never know, I might get lucky," Kelly said wryly. "When Melanie Winters called me for the details of the weekend I'd planned . . ."

"What?" Cole interrupted, stiffening on the stool and fixing Kelly with an arrested expression. "What does Melanie Winters have to do with this?"

"Plenty. She's the president of the Women's Club. She organized most of the event, according to Tessa."

"Who's Tessa?" Cole asked.

"Tessa is the owner of Paperbacks Plus, a bookstore on Main Street just two doors down from Melanie's shop. She also," Trace grinned at the suddenly uncomfortable look on Kelly's face, "is the blonde that Kelly hopes will outbid all the other women for him tomorrow night."

Cole barely registered the information about Tessa. "If Melanie organized this auction, then she'll be there, won't she?" he asked.

"I suppose so," Kelly answered, exchanging a speculative look with Trace.

"What happens after the auction?"

"There's a dinner and a dance—good live band."

"Why?" Trace interrupted, eyeing Cole's preoccupied expression.

Cole glanced at Trace and easily read the shrewd look on his brother's face. His white teeth flashed against tanned skin in a grin that was a replica of Trace's easy smile.

"Because Melanie Winters is a woman I want to get to know better, and I've just spent the last three days trying to figure out a way to see her," his blue gaze flicked to Kelly. "Can anybody buy a ticket to this fund-raiser?"

"Sure," Kelly grinned, amused at the thought of Cole stalemated by a woman. "The more the merrier."

"Good." Cole said with satisfaction.

Trace laughed, and rubbed his forearm across his forehead beneath a twisted blue bandana that held his blonde hair out of his eyes. It left a streak of black grease against his skin. "There must be something about CastleRock women, Cole. If I remember right, I had the same trouble with Lily. Only I used Sarah's wedding as an excuse to see her."

Cole growled an unprintable word at Trace's grinning face and threw his empty soda can at him. He ducked, the can rolling harmlessly and noisily away across the concrete floor.

"Are you and Lily coming to the dinner?" Kelly asked Trace.

"Hell, no," Trace said with a cocky grin. "I've already caught my woman. I don't need to think up excuses to track her down."

"Hah! I'm going to tell her you said that," Cole threatened.

"Don't you dare," Trace groaned. "She'll kill me!"

Cole laughed. He liked his lavender-eyed sister-in-law, and envied Trace his contented happiness. He wanted what Trace and Jesse had with their wives. And maybe, just maybe, he thought, he might find it with Melanie.

"Come on, Melanie, you've got to join in the bidding," Tessa cajoled, her brown eyes dancing with excitement behind huge tortoise-shell glasses. "You're going to miss all the fun!"

Melanie eyed Tessa with fond amusement. The little blonde's curvy figure was draped in a flattering yellow cocktail dress she'd bought at Victoria's Garden months ago in eager anticipation of this evening. From the first time Tessa'd popped her head in the Garden's door to say hello the two had been friends.

"I've already had my fun," she responded, smiling at the air of excitement that fairly vibrated around Tessa. "I've thoroughly enjoyed the months of planning that went into this auction."

"Oh, pooh," Tessa scoffed affectionately. "That's work, not fun! Being president of the CastleRock Business and Professional Women's Club does *not* mean you can't have fun, too. Wouldn't you like to buy one of those gorgeous bachelors for the weekend?"

"No," Melanie smiled to soften the blunt response. The last thing in the world she wanted was to throw away her money for the questionable privilege of spending the weekend with a single man. "Besides, Tessa, there are only twelve bachelors and there must be at least three dozen women who are determined to be the highest bidder on each and every one of them. I wouldn't have a chance against the competition."

"Really?" Just as Melanie had hoped, Tessa's attention was diverted. Her brown eyes held worry for a moment before the little frown smoothed away from between her brows and she smiled again. "I don't care—I'm going to outbid everyone else for Kelly Matthews."

Melanie laughed at the look of determination on her friend's face.

"I hope you . . ."

"Melanie!"

Both Melanie and Tessa turned to see Angie Porter hurrying down the restaurant's plush carpeted hallway toward them.

"What is it?"

"The florist didn't deliver enough flower arrangements and we have six tables without bouquets! What are we going to do?"

With quiet efficiency, Melanie calmed the frazzled redhead, and the three moved off down the hall to the banquet room.

Those few moments chatting with Tessa proved to be the last quiet time Melanie had as she was called upon to solve a rash of last-minute emergencies.

* * *

Two hours later, seated at a front table three steps below the small stage, Melanie heaved a small sigh of relief. The auction had gone well, with good-natured teasing and spontaneous outbreaks of cheers and applause from the crowd as each bachelor was led away by the lucky lady who outbid her competitors.

She glanced over her shoulder at the table behind her and caught Tessa's eye. Tessa winked outrageously at her before smiling with delighted pleasure as Kelly Matthews bent closer to whisper in her ear.

Melanie's stomach rumbled and she quickly clapped a hand over the white silk covering her midriff. A quick glance at the mayor's wife on her left and Angie on her right reassured her that her stomach's complaint had gone unnoticed, and she returned her attention to the stage.

"You've been a wonderful audience, and on behalf of the Business and Professional Women's Association and the Children's Society, who will receive the proceeds from tonight's auction and dinner, I'd like to thank each and every one of you for joining us." Hilary Spencer paused while the audience responded with applause. "I would also like to thank our bachelors . . ." she paused again, smiling while the audience clapped, whistled, and cheered. The twelve men who'd volunteered to be auctioned off laughed and pretended not to be flustered by the attention. Hilary, her silver hair gleaming under the lights, waited patiently for the crowd to settle down, a smile curving her mouth. "I'd also like to extend a special thank-you to a member of our organization, without whose endless hours of hard work this event would not have been possible. Melanie Winters, would you come up here, please?"

Melanie was stunned, and she barely had time to collect her wits before the mayor was pulling back her chair and Angie was urging her to stand.

Cole stood in the back of the big room, leaning one shoulder against the wall just inside the double doors. All the available seating was taken and the standing-room-only crowd lined the wall at the back of the room three persons deep. His searching gaze had found Melanie seated just below the stage shortly after he entered the crowded room. When the mistress of ceremonies called her name and Melanie stood, his gaze sharpened and flew unerringly to her slender figure.

With graceful, fluid movements, she climbed the three shallow steps to the stage. A sleeveless, scoop-necked cocktail dress clung softly to the curves of her body, and her long fall of black hair swung silkily down her back, its glossy ebony highlighted against her tanned skin and white dress.

"Too bad she's not part of the auction. I'd love to buy her for the weekend!"

Cole heard the whispered masculine comment clearly. An instant, possessive anger gripped him and he shot a sharp glance to his right, but there were any number of men who could have uttered the words and he swung his hot-blue gaze back to the stage.

He'd missed the awarding of a plaque. Hilary was enfolding Melanie in a spontaneous hug of affection and appreciation, and all around Cole the crowd broke into applause.

I'd like to buy her for the weekend, too. Cole reflected, his eyes narrowing with sudden inspiration. *Why not?*

Melanie stepped forward, but before she could voice her thanks into the microphone, a deep male voice cut through the expectant silence.

"I'll bid five thousand dollars for Ms. Winters' company for the weekend."

The crowd gasped collectively and swivelled in their seats to gape at the back of the room.

Melanie knew without doubt who owned that deep voice and was instantly furious at his audacity. Her gaze flew over the heads of the seated crowd and found Cole's broad-shouldered figure just as he pushed away from the wall and stood facing her, his hands tucked into the pockets of his slacks, the black tuxedo jacket spread open to reveal the crisp, tucked linen shirt front. He wore the formal evening garb with casual elegance, but there was nothing casual about the intent blue eyes that met hers across the sea of faces.

"I'm sorry," she said calmly, justifiably proud that her voice reflected none of the embarrassed anger that filled her. "But I'm not a part of the auction, Mr. McFadden."

"But this is for charity, Ms. Winters. I'll raise my offer to six thousand."

The men in the audience let out a cheer of encouragement and the women clapped their approval.

"I'm afraid you don't understand, Mr. McFadden," Melanie could feel her cheeks burning with heat and her fingers clenched the engraved plaque so tightly that the brass lettering marked her skin. "The auction was for bachelors, not single women."

Cole smiled, a slow, curving lift of his lips that had every female in the packed room collectively catching their breath and heaving a sigh. One tawny eyebrow lifted in self-deprecation.

"But I don't want to spend the weekend with a bachelor. And since the proceeds go to such a worthy cause, I'll increase my bid to seven thousand."

Once again, the crowd roared their approval, vastly entertained by the tug-of-war going on in front of them.

"Come on, lady!" A male voice yelled from the far side of the room. "Say yes!"

"I'm afraid that's impossible, I . . ." Melanie was interrupted by a frantic tugging on her elbow.

"Melanie!" Hilary whispered, her voice trembling with excitement and disbelief. "Are you crazy? Seven thousand dollars is more money than we made on all the others put together!"

Melanie covered the microphone with one hand and half-turned to look at Hilary.

"I'm not a part of this auction, Hilary!" She whispered vehemently.

"I know that! So what?" Hilary hissed back, her face reflecting her confusion. "It's only one weekend, and the man is *gorgeous*, for heaven's sake!"

Cole watched the two women. Although he couldn't hear what they were saying, it was obvious from their faces that Hilary was urging Melanie to agree and Melanie was refusing.

"I'll raise the bid to ten thousand."

Cole's deep voice interrupted the two women's argument and they turned back to him. Both Melanie and Hilary's faces reflected stunned disbelief.

"Will you stop?" Melanie said, exasperation fraying her customary calm coolness. "No one's bidding against you!"

"So you agree?"

"I didn't say that!" Melanie shot back, beginning to feel trapped.

"Then I'll raise the bid to eleven thousand," he said with unshakable calm.

Melanie stared at Cole and groaned silently. She recognized the stubborn, immovable expression on his face and knew there was no way he was going to give up. Not if he had to stand there all night. Not if she kept saying no forever. Not if it cost him every dime he had.

She tilted her chin and stared at him for a long moment.

The crowd held their breath, their avid gazes flicking from the handsome man at the back of the room to the slender woman on the stage. Had someone dropped a pin, it would have echoed like gunfire in the deathly quiet room.

"The Association will be happy to accept your *very gracious* offer of ten thousand dollars, Mr. McFadden."

The crowd went wild, whistling and cheering. Men slapped Cole on the back in congratulations as he threaded his way among the packed tables and climbed the three steps to the stage. He offered Melanie his arm. Her mouth curved in a smile for the benefit of onlookers, but the gaze that met his was furious and sparked green fire.

"I'm going to kill you for this, Cole McFadden," she whispered angrily.

"If you do, it will still be worth it," he answered. To his relief, she slipped her hand into the crook of his elbow and turned to face the crowd with a calm coolness that he could only admire.

Flashbulbs popped and the crowd cheered and laughed with delight as he escorted her down the steps.

"Thank you, ladies and gentlemen. Now, if you'll adjourn to the banquet room next door, dinner will be served." Hilary's breathless voice came over the microphone and was nearly lost in the noise, but chairs scraped back and people milled about as a general exodus began.

Cole kept Melanie's hand pressed against his side, chaining her to him. He wasn't entirely sure she wouldn't desert him, but he gambled that her sense of fair play would force her, however unwillingly, to spend the weekend with him—starting tonight. He had no doubt that she was furiously angry with him because her slender body was stiff with displeasure. And when the press of the crowd forced their bodies to brush, she went rigid and quickly moved away from him.

"Does it matter where we sit?" he asked, pausing just inside the wide double doors to the banquet room while he scanned the sea of round tables covered with white linen.

"I'd planned to share a table with Hilary and Angie, but the Committee purposely seated each of the high bidders and their bachelors at different tables." She fixed him with a frosty glare. "Since you *bought* me for the evening, I suppose we should sit at one of the tables that wasn't assigned to a high bidder."

Cole shrugged and smiled at her, ignoring her cold stare.

"Great—which one?"

Melanie frowned at him, frustrated at his refusal to respond to her rudeness.

"Why did you do such an insane thing?" she demanded, her voice purposely low to avoid being overheard by the crowd that milled around them.

He didn't bother pretending that he didn't understand what she meant. The blue gaze that met hers darkened to indigo and his arm pressed her hand closer against his ribs.

"I would have paid twice that amount to spend the weekend with you," he said, his voice a deep, rasping murmur.

"Why?" she whispered, green eyes widening with confusion as she stared at him. "There isn't a woman in CastleRock that wouldn't spend the weekend with you—all you have to do is ask."

"Not you. And I don't want any other woman in CastleRock."

"I won't have an affair with you, Cole," she said with soft determination.

"I know," he answered, his blue gaze meeting hers without flinching.

"Then why . . ." she began, unable and unwilling to believe he could have another purpose, but she was interrupted by Kelly and Tessa.

"Hey, Cole!" Kelly clapped a hand on Cole's shoulder and grinned at him before his approving gaze moved to Melanie and back. "You crafty devil, you didn't tell me you were going to turn the tables on the women tonight!"

"I don't tell you everything, Kelly," Cole answered easily, smiling at Tessa as if the intensity of his words to Melanie had never been. "Are you sure you really want to spend two whole days with this guy?"

"Oh, I think so," Tessa slanted a sideways glance at Kelly. "Of course, I've always wanted to learn to fly. When he said he planned a weekend that included flight lessons in his own small plane and flying to New Orleans for dinner and a stroll along Bourbon Street, well . . . I found the idea simply irresistible."

"You found the *idea* irresistible?" Kelly said, chagrined. "And here I thought it was me you found irresistible!"

"Well . . ." Tessa drawled, laughing at the disappointed look on his face. "Let's just say that I'm not sorry you're included in the package."

"Hmmmph," Kelly eyed the curvy little blonde, rapidly revising his earlier opinion. He'd been sure that she was interested in him and he was a little taken aback that he might have been wrong. Intrigued, he narrowed thick lashes over his brown eyes and stared at her.

Tessa met his gaze with an innocent smile, before sliding her hand through the crook of his arm and turning to Melanie.

"We'd better find our seats before we miss dinner," she said, and with a waggle of her finger at Cole, she tugged a fascinated Kelly with her across the room.

Melanie caught the satisfied, knowing wink Tessa gave her and couldn't suppress a small smile.

"I have a feeling Kelly's finally met his match," Cole said.

Melanie glanced up at him to find him watching the couple cross the room, an amused grin curving his mouth.

An answering smile tugged at her lips, but she quickly suppressed it. She didn't want to share even that with him. Determinedly, she pulled her hand from beneath his arm.

"We'd better find a table, too, or Tessa and Kelly aren't the only ones who'll be missing dinner."

Dinner was a test of Melanie's patience and nerves. Not only did she have to endure what seemed like dozens of teasing comments from every male present, but her fellow club members made a point of stopping at her table to offer their laughing congratulations and to be introduced to Cole.

On top of that, the dining tables that were originally meant to seat six had been set for eight in order to accommodate the crush. Melanie found herself sitting so close to Cole that her bare arm brushed against his jacket sleeve and their knees bumped beneath the snowy white tablecloth. When he stretched an arm across the back of her chair and leaned across it to speak to the man seated on her right, she felt surrounded by him.

She turned her head slightly and found his face only inches from hers. His warm breath, scented with after-dinner coffee, stirred her hair at her temples as he spoke. Melanie didn't hear the words, she was too caught up in absorbing the faint aroma of spicy aftershave mingled with the unique scent that was Cole. The heat of his body reached out and enfolded her, stealing her breath and making her heart beat faster. He smiled at something the other man said and his teeth flashed whitely against tanned skin, his eyes narrowing and crinkling with tiny laugh lines at the corners. She resisted the urge to stroke his cheek with her fingertip.

Cole glanced down at Melanie and his breath caught in his throat. Her green eyes were unguarded, and he felt the weight of her gaze as surely as if she'd reached out a hand and touched him before she dropped her lashes, effectively concealing her thoughts.

"Dance with me," he said softly, his lips barely brushing her ear.

"I don't think that's a good idea," she managed to get out, unable to move away from him.

"Why not?" he murmured. His hand left the back of her chair and lifted to finger a strand of her hair, his knuckles grazing her skin where her dress left her shoulder blades bare.

"Because, I . . ." she closed her eyes, fighting her body's inclination to sway against the solid bulk of his.

Cole knew her will struggled against her need. Before her head overruled her heart, he moved quickly. His hand left her hair and moved in a warm caress down her bare arm to catch her fingers in his.

"You think too much," he muttered, and stood, pulling her up beside him.

Melanie tried to tug her hand from his but his grip was too firm, and short of digging in her heels and shouting at him, there was little she could do. Reluctant to provide further entertainment for the crowd, she gave up and followed him. But when he stopped and pulled her into his arms on the dimly lit dance floor, she was stiff and uncooperative.

"Uh–oh," Cole tipped his head to look down into her face, allowing her the foot of space she seemed determined to keep between their bodies. "You're mad again, aren't you?"

"Still," she said pointedly, glaring at him. "I am angry, *still.* And I am probably going to continue to be angry with you until you stop embarrassing me and dragging me around!"

"I'm sorry, honey," he said. "But I told you I was going to find a way to prove to you that I'm not dangerous. And I couldn't do that if you kept refusing to spend time with me. Most women would be flattered if a man was willing to pay ten thousand dollars to spend the weekend with them. And as for dragging you around, I . . ."

"I am *not* most women," Melanie hissed, her eyes shooting green sparks at him.

"I know you're not," he said softly, his own blue eyes going hot with need. "You're the only woman."

Speechless, Melanie could only stare at him. Just

when she was ready to kill him, he would say something that made her doubt everything she knew to be true about him. All the antagonism drained from her body.

"Let's not fight. Can't we declare a truce for the weekend?" he asked, his deep voice a quiet rumble against her ear as he gently pulled her resisting body against his.

Melanie closed her eyes against a wave of emotion.

"Cole, I don't think . . ." she began in a voice that had lost its conviction.

". . . that's it's a good idea. Yeah, I know." His voice held wry amusement. "But can't we agree to a truce, anyway?"

It was suddenly very difficult to stay angry at him. Melanie felt her traitorous body swaying involuntarily toward his and his arms gathered her closer.

"All right, we'll declare a truce," she responded softly. "But you have to promise to be a gentleman," she added with a sudden infusion of determination.

"Oh, absolutely," he vowed solemnly. "I'll be a complete gentleman."

There was something about the tone of his voice that made her wonder if she should believe him, but when she tipped her head back and frowned up at him, his blue eyes met hers with guileless innocence.

Melanie wasn't convinced, but since she was stuck with him for the weekend, even an empty promise was better than none.

FOUR

It was after one a.m. before Cole drove her home and walked her up the sidewalk to her front door. The 1950s' era bungalow had a single lamp lit in the living room and its faint glow through the drapes provided welcoming warmth. It was the only window that wasn't dark on the quiet residential street.

The muggy heat that had weighted the evening before had been stripped away by the chill of early morning, and the cool brush of air against Melanie's skin raised goosebumps.

It's just the chilly air, she assured herself silently, her palms rubbing her arms to warm them beneath the folds of her fringed floral shawl. *I'm not the least bit nervous about being alone with Cole McFadden!*

Cole walked beside Melanie, scrupulously keeping a twelve-inch space between their bodies. But despite the distance that separated them, he was achingly aware of her slender curved shape outlined by wrapped floral silk, shimmering with ghostly paleness against the darkness. The scent of her perfume drifted to tease his nostrils with each movement she made. Her heels clicked against the sidewalk, his own footsteps making a deeper, more solid echo in the early morning hush.

Silently, they climbed the steps to her porch and crossed the painted white boards to the door, where Cole held open the outer screen and took the house key from her cold fingers. He pushed open the heavy oak inner door and Melanie stepped over the threshold, turning to face him with nervous apprehension.

"So," Cole cleared his throat, suddenly feeling like a fifteen-year-old on his first date. "I'll pick you up around ten tomorrow morning, if that's all right?"

"That's fine," Melanie answered, unconsciously twining the mauve fringe of the shawl through her fingers. "Where are we going?"

"Out to the lake. Dad has a cabin cruiser docked at Larson's Resort and we can water ski and swim, if you'd like, and have a picnic."

Melanie's heart lurched. She'd rather be boiled in oil than spend the day on the lake with him, for it would constantly remind her of other, happier summer days. But if she refused, he was sure to demand to know why and she couldn't tell him the memories were still too painful.

"That should be fun," she lied, forcing her gaze to meet his without flinching. "I could use a relaxing day on the water."

"Great," Cole responded, searching the green eyes that gazed into his. Although her face was composed and calm, a vulnerable confusion flickered in the depths of her eyes, together with an unconscious plea that touched his heart. "Well . . ." he shrugged and held out his hand. Her house key nestled on its silver ring in his palm and when Melanie's fingers closed over it, he gently trapped her hand in his much bigger one. Her lashes flicked quickly up and her gaze flew to meet his. Once again, Cole caught a faint look of alarm before her expression went carefully watchful and cool.

The hand within his was soft and small, infinitely feminine against his own calloused palm, but Cole resisted the urge to pull her closer and cover her mouth with his to take the deep, wet kiss his body craved. Instead, he held her hand carefully within his own and bent forward to brush a gentle kiss against her forehead.

"I'll see you in the morning," he murmured, releasing her fingers and stepping back to let the screen door swing shut between them. "Ten o'clock."

With a last glance that swept her from her toes to the crown of her head, he turned on his heel and left the porch, loping down the steps and the sidewalk to his car.

Melanie leaned her forehead against the doorjamb and let her body go slack against its support. He hadn't kissed her, except for that warm brush of lips against her forehead, and she wasn't sure if she was glad or disappointed.

* * *

Cole bounded up the steps, crossed her porch with impatient strides, and rapped his knuckles against the door, making the screen rattle under the quick strokes. Would she keep her part of the bargain and spend the day with him? Or had she spent the night reconsidering and deciding to stand him up?

The door swung inward and Cole's taut muscles relaxed with relief, the frown that pulled down his brows fading as his gaze swept over her with lightning quickness.

"Hi," he grinned, delighted with the view of her tanned, shapely legs left bare by white shorts. The emerald green of a one-piece bathing suit was visible through the thin white cotton of an oversize man's shirt, which was tucked in and bloused out over the waistband of the shorts. The long sleeves were folded back to her elbows, the collar turned up to frame her face, and her long hair was pulled back into a ponytail. She looked young and innocently uncomplicated, until his gaze met hers. Those emerald eyes were anything but uncomplicated, and they held secrets and a trace of wariness that stymied him. He'd promised to be on his best behavior, but evidently she still didn't trust him. He ruthlessly restrained the urge to yank open the screen door, pick her up, and find the nearest flat surface to make love to her. "Are you ready to go?"

"Yes," she said, thankful that she had the edge of the open door to support her. He was wearing a white tank top and worn jeans that were indecently tight, his feet shoved into tattered white canvas sneakers without laces. She forced her gaze up to meet his and away from the expanse of sleek, tanned muscles that sculpted his chest and defined his arms. That was a mistake because the heat in his blue eyes was as distracting as his body. She dragged her gaze away from his and forced herself to leave the support of the door. "I'm ready—just let me get my bag."

She left the doorway and disappeared for a moment. Then she was back, and Cole held open the screen door while she bent her head to lock the inner door.

She smells like summer flowers, Cole thought absently, nostrils flaring to inhale her scent while his eyes lingered on the vulnerable curve of her nape. Silky black wisps of hair escaped the ponytail holder and brushed against soft skin. Before he could follow his first instinct and bend to test the softness of skin and silky hair with his lips, she straightened and turned. Her green eyes widened when she saw the brief inches that separated their bodies. Cole immediately stepped back and was rewarded by a smile of relief that lit her eyes and curved her mouth.

He tugged the straw tote bag from her fingers and she moved ahead of him down the steps to the sidewalk, only to stop dead still and stare with surprised delight at the car that sat in her driveway.

"Oh, my goodness! Is this yours?"

"Nope, it's my dad's," Cole opened the trunk of the turquoise and white 1959 Thunderbird and squeezed her bag in next to the wicker hamper and blankets that nearly filled the small trunk. "Do you like it?" He slammed the trunk lid and moved back to open the passenger door for her.

"I love it!" Melanie's gaze moved appreciatively over the gleaming classic car. Its white canvas convertible top was folded back and buttoned under a white leather cover. The body was small and sporty, the waxed and polished turquoise and white paint and the silver chrome wheels gleaming under the hot mid-morning sun. She slid into the low-slung car and stroked an appreciative hand over the leather seat, glancing sideways at Cole as he pulled open the driver's door and levered himself beneath the wheel. "Why are you driving your father's car?"

"Because I flew home from Atlanta, I didn't drive," he shot her a sideways glance as he turned the key in the ignition. He didn't tell her that he couldn't have driven his black Porsche because the strain of depressing the powerful clutch to shift the transmission over the long miles between Atlanta and CastleRock would have been impossible with his injured leg.

"So, you're here without a car?"

"Sort of," Cole grinned wryly at her, twisting to stretch his arm out along the seat behind her as he reversed out of the driveway and into the street. "Dad's been keeping my '56 Chevy that I drove in high school up on blocks in his garage for me. I've been fiddling around with it since I've been home, getting it street-legal again."

Melanie rested her arm along the door and relaxed against the sun-warmed leather as Cole faced forward again and shifted the automatic transmission into gear. The breeze stirred by their passing lifted his hair away from his face, ruffling the thick tawny strands. The black sunglasses he'd slipped on his nose hid his eyes from her view, but her observant gaze still read a restrained restlessness in his big body.

"You've been bored since you got back, haven't you?" she asked.

Cole flicked her a sideways glance before turning his attention back to traffic.

"Not bored, exactly," his broad shoulders lifted in a shrug, the powerful muscles rippling beneath the brief tank top. "It's just that I'm used to a tight schedule with demands on my time that never stop. It's hard to adjust to the sudden switch to complete rest, with nothing but time on my hands to fill."

"I suppose that once you're used to the fast lane, life away from it must seem very dull," she murmured, absentmindedly noting the outskirts of CastleRock as they quickly left the broad, tree-shaded residential streets for the two-lane blacktop that circled the lake.

Cole's hands closed over the steering wheel with a punishing grip.

"That depends on what you mean by the fast lane," he said tightly. "If you're referring to twelve-hour workdays spent in the garage or the office, midnight meetings to work on race strategy, eighteen-hour commutes from one race track to another in a van and trailer, followed by six to eight gruelling hours manhandling a car around a track at two hundred miles an hour, then, yeah, it's hard to get used to life away from that."

Melanie stared at him, completely taken aback.

"No," she said slowly, eyeing him, "that's not what I meant. I meant the glamour—the parties, the adoration of the fans, the beauty queens, and the track groupies."

"I'm not denying that's a part of professional racing," Cole conceded, wincing inwardly at the swift flash of disapproval and well-bred disgust that moved across her expressive face. "But it's optional and most race car drivers burn the candle at both ends when they're young. Then they either burn-out or wise-up, fall in love, get married and have kids, just like most of the rest of the male population in the United States."

"And live happily ever after?" Melanie asked skeptically.

"Most of the time," he nodded in agreement. "Sometimes not." He flashed a glance at her and found her watching him with a tiny frown pulling down the dark arch of her brows as she considered his words. "But that's true of any cross section of people in any profession in the United States. Sometimes marriage works, sometimes it doesn't."

"I hate that attitude," she said with sudden fierceness, glaring at him.

"What attitude?"

"That attitude—shrugging off marriage vows and promises of forever as if commitment were an outdated concept that only works as long as life is easy!"

"I didn't know you felt so strongly about keeping promises and vows," he said sardonically, shooting her a sideways glance as he braked and slowed at the entrance to Larson's Resort.

"Well, I do," Melanie said softly, tilting her chin stubbornly. How dare he remind her so casually of how little promises of forever meant to him.

"This is wonderful," Melanie sighed, surprising herself.

"Yeah," Cole smiled contentedly, eyes closed.

They lay side by side on an old quilt beneath the shade of an oak tree, the remains of their picnic lunch strewn on the grass beside them. The mid-afternoon sun slanted through the thick leafy canopy above them, dappling their faces with a shifting pattern of hot sun and cool shade. Melanie's hands were folded contentedly over the damp green swimsuit covering her midriff, while Cole's were stacked beneath his head. Somewhere in the leafy copse behind them, a bee buzzed, the sound a fitting accompaniment to the lazy somnolence of the afternoon.

"How long has it been since you spent a Saturday just being lazy?" Cole asked without opening his eyes.

Melanie was silent for a long moment while she thought about that.

"Goodness," she said with slow surprise, "you know, it's been so long that I can't remember!"

"You work too hard," Cole commented.

"*I* work too hard!" Melanie rolled her head sideways against the quilt to look at him. "You're the one who said you were having trouble adjusting to days without constant pressures and demands on your time!''

''True,'' A lazy grin curved his mouth. ''But I've had six weeks of recuperating and doing nothing but lying around.''

''Hmm,'' Melanie commented, averting her gaze from the expanse of sleek, tanned muscles visible above and below the faded cut-off jeans that served as his bathing trunks. She stared up at the leafy branches that shaded them.

Cole slitted open one eye and stared at her consideringly. The damp green bathing suit was modest, but it had French-cut legs and dropped to just below her waist in back. Earlier, it had taken all his will power to keep from staring openmouthed when she shed her shorts and shirt before going over the edge of the boat and into the lake. She was as slender and well-shaped as she had been as a teen-ager, but there was a mature ripeness in the slightly fuller curves of breasts and hips that made his mouth go dry and his palms itch.

''Is that all you have to say? *Hmmm?*'' he teased, rolling on his side and propping himself up on one elbow while he rested his cheek against his fist. ''What have you been doing on Saturdays that is more important than lying in the grass listening to the bees and crickets?''

Melanie left her contemplation of the green canopy high above them and turned her head to look at him. ''Working at the shop. Saturday is our busiest day of the week, and we stay open late at night.''

"What about Sundays?" he asked, curious about this glimpse into her life.

"Sunday mornings I go to church and then have lunch with my parents," she answered, wondering why he was so interested in the mundane details of her life. "In the afternoon, I usually go back to the shop to do paper work."

"No wonder you aren't as tan as I remembered you being in the summer," he commented, and without thinking, he stretched out a forefinger and traced a slow path from her knee up her thigh. "You don't have time to get out in the sun."

"No, I don't." Agitated, Melanie sat upright, shifting her leg away from the brush of his finger. She gazed around the little cove where they sat. The lake water lapped gently at the small sandy beach, and offshore the cabin cruiser rocked easily at anchor. Dotted with scattered oaks, elms, and the infrequent white bark of a birch tree, the land sloped gently upward and away from the half-moon of beach where they lay. "I think I'll take a walk to work off lunch. Otherwise, I'll be tempted to sleep the afternoon away."

"Sounds like a good idea." Cole didn't miss her agitation, nor the quick removal of her leg from his touch. He rolled to his feet and held out his hand. "I'll go with you."

Silently, Melanie took his hand and let him pull her to her feet, but she slipped her fingers from his the moment she was upright, using the pretext of looking for her sandals to put distance between them.

Well aware of her evasion, Cole waited patiently

for her, until she slipped the sandal's brown leather soles and narrow straps on her feet.

"There's a path we can take," he gestured to a worn trail visible through the uncut shaggy grass. "It leads across the empty lots to the highway. There's a fork in the trail about two-thirds of the way to the road that curves around to the Connors' property on the south and then follows the property line back to the lake."

Melanie moved ahead of him and up the path. A pair of chipmunks raced for the protection of an oak tree at their approach, darting up the rough trunk only to halt halfway up to look back and chatter their displeasure at being disturbed. She paused to watch them, laughing at their bright black eyes and noisy irritation.

"Aren't they cute?" Melanie looked back over her shoulder at Cole, her own eyes bright with delight at the little animals' antics.

"Yeah," Cole said, grinning back at her. "Reminds me of the Chip and Dale cartoons I used to watch when I was a kid."

"I loved those, too." Her green eyes warm with shared remembrance, Melanie once again felt the tug of an attraction that was more than physical. She'd forgotten, or refused to remember, that they'd shared more than an overwhelming physical attraction. She'd loved every moment they'd spent together that long-ago summer. And when it ended, she'd mourned more than the loss of the incredible physical satisfaction she'd found with Cole. She'd lost the feeling of being completed and whole. Abruptly, she wrenched her thoughts away from her memories and turned to move forward along the path.

Cole walked silently beside her, wondering what thoughts had wiped the smile from her lips and chased shadows across her green eyes.

"Oh, look! Wild roses," she stopped and bent forward to sniff, closing her eyes with pleasure as she inhaled the fragrance. She glanced up and found Cole watching her. "They always smell so much stronger than hybrids," she commented, suddenly nervous. Her gaze shifted away from him and moved over the grassy knoll where they stood. The path they had just travelled wound its lazy way down the incline and disappeared at the edge of the lake where the grass gave way to the strip of sand. She was suddenly aware of how isolated they were in the sun-drenched woods, with only the trees and the tangle of rosebushes for an audience. "Maybe we should go back to the lake," she said abruptly, glancing nervously around again. If there were neighbors, she couldn't hear them, nor could she see roof lines through the trees.

"Why?" Cole asked, his own eyes following hers.

"Because we're trespassing."

"No, we're not," his deep voice held calm assurance.

"How do you know?" she asked curiously, her gaze drawn back to his face. "Do you know the owners?"

"You might say that," he smiled down at her. "These three acres are mine."

"Yours?" Melanie was stunned. "You mean you

own all of this?'' her hand swept in a half-circle that covered the land that lay between them and the lake.

''Yup,'' he said, his gaze moving with possessive pride over the land before them, ''and everything between us and the highway.''

''Why?'' she asked, nonplussed.

''Why?'' he looked at her, confused. ''Why not? Don't you want to own land someday?''

''Of course, I suppose everyone does. But I meant, why here?''

''Why not here? CastleRock is my hometown.''

''I know, but,'' she paused, staring at him in confusion, ''but you don't live here.''

''I will, someday, when I retire from racing,'' he said with quiet certainty, his blue gaze leaving hers to move slowly over the sun-and-shade dappled meadow. ''I'm going to build my house right here, so I can sit on the front porch and see the trees and the land sloping down to the lake. I want a boat, too, so I can go fishing whenever I want.''

''I just can't believe that you would ever quit racing and come back to live in CastleRock,'' Melanie shook her head in amazement.

''Why not?''

''Well, because . . .'' she paused, searching for words. ''It's just difficult to believe that you would ever give up the excitement and glamour of racing for quiet life in a small town.''

Cole shrugged, his eyes narrowing as he tried to read her face.

''I've always known that sooner or later I'd stop driving race cars. I'm more interested these days in other aspects—such as building engines and designing the perfect car. Besides,'' his thick lashes narrowed further to conceal his thoughts, ''the racing circuit is no place to raise a family.''

Melanie nearly gasped aloud at the blinding pain that stole her breath and squeezed her chest. A family? He was getting married? For one long moment, she could only stare at him blankly while she struggled to absorb the blow.

''No,'' she said with commendable calm, her voice carefully expressionless, ''no, I suppose it's not.''

Cole couldn't tell from her expression what reaction, if any, she had to his mentioning a family. He plucked a rose from the bush and absentmindedly began to strip the thorns from the pale green stem.

''But CastleRock is the perfect place to raise kids,'' he said. ''Do you remember the children we talked about having?'' his eyes lifted to fasten intently on hers, and were met by a flash of such pain and torment he instinctively reached out to hold and comfort her.

Melanie stepped back, evading his touch, her own arms wrapping protectively around her middle as if to shield herself from him.

''Yes,'' she said shakily, forcing her eyes not to drop from his, forcing her feet not to turn and run, taking her away from him. ''I remember. I remember that we were very young and that lust and hormones made us say a lot of things that neither of us meant.''

Her sword thrust hit home and Cole winced. Only the fever bright pain in her eyes kept him from responding with all the bitter anger that still festered whenever he thought of how quickly she had forgotten her summer promises of forever. He clamped down on his anger and reminded himself that this was another time, another place, and another chance—maybe their last.

His broad shoulders lifted in a shrug of dismissal.

"Maybe you're right," he said noncommittally, neither agreeing nor disagreeing, "but we're old enough now to know how we feel about a family. How about you, Melanie, do you want to have kids?"

"No," her response was quick and defensive. "I never want to have children."

Cole was stunned.

"I can't believe that," he said with slow shock. "You dreamed about having children—you even had names picked out for them."

"That was a long time ago. Now I don't plan to be a mother."

"What about when you get married? What if your husband wants children?" Cole asked slowly.

"Since I don't plan to marry, the question will never arise," Melanie answered. She could tell by the stunned surprise on Cole's handsome face that he wasn't satisfied by her answers. Before he could voice the next question that obviously trembled on the tip of his tongue, she forestalled him by asking one of her own. "What about your fiancée? Does she want children?"

"Fiancée? What fiancée?" Cole was still struggling to accept that the Melanie he'd known, who had adored children, had become a woman who clearly was adamantly opposed to the thought of having babies. "I'm not engaged." A perplexed frown pulled down his tawny brows. "Where did you get that idea?"

Melanie stared at the confused look on his handsome face. Had she jumped to the wrong conclusion?

"You said you planned to have children—I assumed that you were getting married." A sudden thought occurred to her. "Unless, of course, you plan to have them without getting married."

Cole stared at her for a moment before her meaning sank in. His confused frown dissolved into a grin that twitched at his lips and then broadened until his teeth flashed whitely against tan skin. The corners of his eyes crinkled, his blue eyes dancing with amusement.

"No, ma'am," he drawled. "Just to set the record straight, I am not engaged, I am not living in sin and producing illegitimate children, and I have no plans to do so. *If* I am lucky enough to find the right woman and *if* I am lucky enough to have her say yes, then I'll marry her. And then, *if* we're lucky, we'll have children."

Melanie stared at him consideringly. He seemed perfectly sincere, but she wondered if she could trust his teasing tone. *Besides,* she thought with despair, *I shouldn't be feeling this immense relief that he isn't marrying someone else. Why should I care? He's still off-limits to me. This doesn't change anything.* She forced a smile and turned away to the path. "I'm glad to hear that—I'm sure your mother will be pleased. It's awfully warm,'' she said with an abrupt change of subject. ''I'd love to cool off in the water. Are you coming?'' She tossed the last question over her shoulder, but her green eyes refused to meet his.

What the hell happened to you in the eight years I've been gone, green eyes? Cole watched the swing of the glossy-black ponytail against her nape as she moved ahead of him down the trail. She wasn't running, but she moved just quickly enough to keep ahead of him. He allowed it, knowing that he'd unwittingly raised a painful subject and caused her grief. *Where did the warm, open, loving girl go and why do you feel the need to protect your heart so fiercely.* He shook his head unbelievingly. *Not have children? My god, I can't imagine anyone who would make a better mother.*

Melanie half ran down the path, kicked off her sandals, and waded into the cool, green lake.

If I can just get through this weekend—she thought, swimming with determined strokes toward the anchored Bayliner. *He'll be going back to Georgia soon, and I probably won't see him for another eight years!*

But the thought wasn't comforting. Instead, knowing he would move on and leave her again only left a bleak coldness that weighted her heart.

She reached the boat and caught the bottom rung of the ladder, pausing to catch her breath.

''I'll race you to the Connors' dock.''

Cole's deep voice behind her startled her, and she spun to look over her shoulder. He was treading water not three feet away from her, droplets of moisture sparkling on his lashes and turning the tawny streaks in his blond hair to dark gold. The blue eyes fixed on hers held only friendly invitation. And, reassured by his return to the determinedly neutral friendliness he'd displayed during the hours they'd spent together, Melanie smiled back at him.

"If I get a head start," she said.

"How much of a head start?" he asked, thick eyelashes narrowing consideringly over his eyes.

"Half the length of a football field," she responded promptly.

"What! That's highway robbery!" he protested. "I tell you what, you can have fifty feet."

"How far is that?"

Cole groaned and rolled his eyes.

"Woman, you're as bad as the females in my family! They have no concept of distance!"

"I do, too," Melanie said loftily. "I just use more practical reference points than yardsticks."

"Okay, okay," Cole glanced around him, then eyed the Bayliner with sudden inspiration. "You can have two-and-a-half boat lengths for a lead. That's approximately fifty feet."

Melanie ran a measuring eye down the length of the sleek craft.

"Done," she nodded decisively and kicked away from the Bayliner's ladder.

She swam with measured strokes, conserving her strength until she heard Cole begin to swim behind her. Then she concentrated on the race and by the time Cole pulled alongside of her, they were nearly within touching distance of the dock. Although she put on a burst of speed, he still easily outdistanced her.

"What took you so long?" he asked teasingly, laughing down at her as she held on to the edge of the wooden dock and took in lungs full of air, her breasts rising and falling beneath the wet emerald green material with each quick breath she took. He reached out a hand and brushed a clinging tendril of wet, black-silk hair from her cheek and tucked it behind her ear.

Melanie caught her breath, her eyes widening with shock as she went completely still under his touch.

"Hey," his voice was whisper soft and held a note of frustration. "Relax—I'm not going to do anything you don't want, Melanie. You've been as skittish as a deer with a hunter on her trail all day long. Every time I touch you, you freeze. I'm not an axe murderer or a convicted rapist."

"I know," she said huskily. How could she tell him that she was far more afraid of her body's reactions to his casual touching than she was of him? "It's just that I don't think . . ."

"You don't think it's safe or wise for us to see each other," he grimaced with self-derision. "Yeah, I know, honey. You keep saying that."

Melanie flushed self-consciously.

"I'm suppose you think I'm overreacting, but . . ."

Cole laid a finger over her lips, silencing her.

"No, I don't. But I wish you'd stop worrying about spending time with me and just relax and enjoy yourself. Didn't we declare a truce for the weekend?"

"Yes."

Her soft lips moving under his sensitive fingertip nearly undid Cole's determination to keep this light and reassuring.

"So, stop thinking I'm going to jump your bones any second. Not that the idea isn't appealing, mind you," he added, a wicked grin spreading slowly across his handsome features, "but I'll wait until you're so charmed and fascinated by me that you decide to jump my bones."

Melanie couldn't help it. She laughed reluctantly, her green eyes softening and warming.

"Then I have nothing to worry about," she said wryly, smiling at his shrug of disappointment. She pushed away from the dock and swam leisurely toward the cruiser, turning to float on her back and watch him until she was satisfied with the expanse of water that separated them. "Race you back to the boat," she called and swiftly turned, moving through the water with fast, efficient strokes.

"Hey!" Startled, Cole kicked away from the dock and surged through the water after her.

FIVE

"Where would you like to have dinner?" Cole asked. He slid beneath the steering wheel and turned to look at Melanie. Her cheeks and the bridge of her nose were pink from the sun, and she'd rinsed her hair beneath the Resort's dockside shower to rid it of lake water. The damp strands spread across her shoulders, gleaming wetly black beneath the westward slanting sun. Dressed once again in the white shirt and shorts, and with only a bare minimum of makeup on her fine-boned features, she looked about eighteen years old.

"Anywhere—as long as it's fast," she said. "I'm starved."

"Do you want to go home and change and go somewhere nice? We could go to the Lakeshore—but not dressed like this."

Melanie considered it for a moment before shaking her head.

"No—I'm too lazy to change and too hungry to wait. Isn't there someplace that will let us in dressed as we are?"

Cole glanced down at his faded, ripped jeans and blue T-shirt with the racing logo across the front, then back at her.

"You could get in anywhere, but the way I'm dressed limits our possibilities." Thoughtfully, he squinted his eyes against the westernly sun. "We could go to Big Eddie's Truck Stop and get hamburgers—or Eddie does a mean chicken-fried steak."

"Steak sounds wonderful!"

"Then steak it is," Cole backed the Thunderbird out of the parking lot and headed back to town.

By the time they reached CastleRock, it was nearly dusk. Carloads of teen-agers gathered in groups under the neon lights of the drive-in restaurant and cruised up and down Main Street. A passing carload of high-school boys whistled and yelled words of admiration at the classic convertible Thunderbird, and Cole grinned and lifted his hand in acknowledgment.

By the time they reached Big Eddie's and pulled into the parking lot, they'd run a gauntlet of whistles from boys and sighs from girls. Melanie slid out of the low-slung car and laughed up at Cole.

"I'm not sure which the girls liked the most—the car or you!"

Cole grimaced, and to Melanie's surprise, a flush moved up his throat and stained his cheeks.

"It was the car, not me," he said with a dismissing shrug, and caught her arm to turn her toward the glass doors of the cafe.

Melanie moved ahead of him, hiding an amused smile. After surviving the media attention generated by his high-profile career, his obvious embarrassment at the shrieks and sighs from the young girls was unexpected and endearing.

Cole pulled open the heavy glass door to the Truck Stop and they stepped inside, halting abruptly while they searched the crowded room for vacant seats. The long counter, with its red vinyl stools, was fully occupied and most of the square tables between the counter and the wall were too. The high-backed booths lining the outer walls all held diners.

"Cole . . ." Melanie glanced over her shoulder at him and her voice faltered and trailed off into silence when she found him standing close behind her, his chest nearly touching her shoulders and his face only inches above hers.

"Hmmmm?" His gaze left its sweeping search of the room and dropped down to hers. For a long moment, the clatter of crockery, the chatter and laughter of the crowd, and the Charlie Daniels tune from the jukebox in the corner all faded away while they stood motionless, blue gaze locked with green.

"Excuse me," a voice said loudly at Cole's back. "Excuse me?"

With a start, he glanced away from Melanie to find a couple in their mid-fifties patiently waiting for them to move out of the doorway.

"Sorry," he murmured. His hand slipped to Melanie's waist and he gently urged her ahead of him, while he once again scanned the crowded cafe. This time, he was rewarded by the sight of three young women sliding out of a booth across the room. "There's an empty booth," he bent forward to say in Melanie's ear. "Let's grab it before somebody else does."

Melanie nodded in agreement. She slid onto the red Naugahyde seat with relief, the spot where his hand had rested against her waist warm from his touch. Fortunately for her composure, a harried waitress arrived immediately and cleared the table, quickly taking their order before she rushed off.

"Saturday night is a busy night at Big Eddie's," Cole observed, glancing around at the casually dressed throng that crowded the restaurant. Truckers in boots and jeans, families in shorts and sandals accompanying boys in dirt-stained Little League uniforms, and suntanned teen-agers in cut-off jeans pulled on over their still-damp bathing suits, filled the tables, booths, and the counter stools. "Some things never change."

"Mm-hmm," Melanie agreed, her own gaze flicking over the busy cafe. "Looks like the CastleRock Astros won their game tonight."

Cole's glance followed hers to a table where four little boys in dirty uniforms and baseball caps sat with their parents and ate hamburgers, their smudged faces reflecting the glow of victory and a certain swaggering pride.

"Boy, does that bring back memories," he chuckled, blue eyes warm with remembrance as he looked at the freckled, sunburned faces.

"Did you play Little League baseball?" Melanie asked.

"Oh, yeah," Cole replied, "and the coach always brought us to Big Eddie's for hamburgers after a game, win or lose. But it was always more fun if we'd won the game and could rehash all the brilliant plays we'd made."

"Do you do the same thing after a race?" she asked curiously, watching him over the rim of her water glass as she sipped.

Cole laughed, slanting her a rueful look.

"How did you know?" he asked.

"Just a guess," she smiled back, lost in the warm depths of his blue eyes that darkened with an emotion that wasn't quite lust.

"Here's your order, folks."

Melanie was relieved at the waitress's interruption, for it broke the spell that wrapped around them. She dropped her lashes, concealing her eyes and the emotion that she was afraid Cole could read too easily in their green depths, and concentrated on the sizzling steak.

An hour later, after lingering over after-dinner coffee, Melanie stood beside Cole while he paid for their dinner at the cash register, and swallowed a sigh as she watched him shove his hand into his jeans pocket to pull out folded bills. The movement strained the worn denim below his belt and Melanie forced her fascinated eyes away from his body.

It's just lust, she told herself firmly. *The only rea-*

son I'm reacting like this is because we were once intimate.

Cole tucked his money back into his pocket and looked down at Melanie. Half of his precious weekend with her was nearly over and he was reluctant to let the evening end so soon. A burst of laughter from the tavern connected to the Truck Stop's restaurant sounded through the joining door, and he brightened with sudden inspiration.

"It's too early to go home," he said, his gaze moving with intent absorption over her features. "Let's go next door and dance. Come on," he said teasingly as her green eyes shaded with troubled indecision. "I'll buy you a beer and even let you pick three out of every five songs on the jukebox."

Melanie only hesitated a moment. The reality was that she, too, didn't want the evening to end, even though she knew this weekend was an isolated forty-eight hours out of time. Come Monday morning, she would have to return to her solitary life. Although she knew she was falling more under his spell by the hour, she still couldn't resist the temptation to lengthen the time with him.

"All right," She was rewarded by a smile of delighted pleasure that lit Cole's face, "but only if *I* get to choose *all* the music! None of that country-western stuff you used to listen to!"

"What!" Cole grinned down at her and caught her hand, threading her slim fingers through his calloused ones. "You don't like country music?"

"Sometimes," she conceded, allowing him the small,

intimate gesture of possession without protest, "but sometimes it's just too sad."

"Mmmmh," Cole agreed, holding open the door to the tavern so she could walk ahead of him. "An Alabama friend of mine swears there're only three kinds of country songs—they're either sighin', cryin', or leavin' town."

Melanie laughed. "I have to agree with your friend."

Two hours later, Melanie stood locked in Cole's arms, swaying slowly to the sound of Patsy Cline crooning the lyrics to "Crazy" from the neon-lit jukebox in the corner of the tavern. They'd started out dancing a careful distance apart, but the inches between them narrowed and then disappeared under the lure of the music, the dim lights, and the undeniable yearning each felt.

Cole's barely mended leg ached, and he knew it was late and he should take her home. But he couldn't bring himself to release her. It felt so good to hold her. The snug fit of her body leaning trustingly against his, the solid lock of his hands at her waist, and her arms around his neck soothed the deep, lonely ache in his heart that he'd grown so accustomed to living with over the years that he'd almost learned to ignore it.

Melanie refused to think about the consequences and gave herself up to the sheer comforting pleasure of being held. It wasn't that she hadn't danced with any male since Cole left. She had, but this was less like dancing and more like being hugged, loved, and cuddled. Cole's hands stroked slowly up and down her back, in caresses that turned her bones to rubber and brought every nerve in her body to tingling, aching awareness. With each step they took, his long legs encased in worn denim shifted against her own, bare beneath the hem of her shorts, and the repeated, stroking contact was powerfully seductive, shortening her breath and sending her heartbeat thudding against her ribs.

"It's late," Cole's voice sounded reluctantly, huskily, against her ear. "I suppose I'd better take you home."

"Mmmmh," Melanie murmured, barely aware of his words.

Cole tipped his head back and looked down at her. The green eyes that lifted drowsily to meet his reflected the same drugged arousal that gripped him. He tensed, his body surging with instant response. He struggled to remember he'd vowed to spend the weekend getting to know the woman she'd become, and convincing her he wanted more than just a physical relationship. His arms contracted, pressing her tightly against him and he groaned inwardly, his eyes squeezed shut while he battled for control.

Startled from her sensual lethargy, Melanie felt the hard muscles of his body tense as Cole crushed her close. It was impossible not to be aware that he was just as affected by their contact as she was. A small feminine smile of satisfaction curved her lips, a part of her rejoicing that she aroused him with the same intensity he evoked in her. But a small, nagging voice in the back of her mind insistently reminded her that their mutual attraction was dangerous, that it would take very little for it to explode into a raging fire beyond her control. It was a sobering thought and when the hard arms that enfolded her relaxed and Cole released her, she didn't protest.

Gone was the sensual absorption from the green eyes lifted to his. Instead, there was a cautious wariness in the emerald depths. Although he hated to see it, Cole couldn't deny her right to feel wary of the heat that flared between them. He slid an arm around her shoulders and tucked her against his side.

"If I don't get you home, Cinderella," he murmured throatily, smiling down into her wide green eyes, "you'll sleep tomorrow away and I'll lose my last twenty-four hours with you."

"I wouldn't sleep through tomorrow," Melanie protested as they left the tavern and walked to the car.

"No?" Cole glanced down at her. The moonlight threw intriguing shadows across her face, accentuating the smudges of tiredness beneath her eyes. He wondered fleetingly if she'd spent as many wakeful hours struggling to sleep as he had over the last few days. "If I remember correctly, you need ten hours of sleep a night or else you're cranky and grouchy the next day. I don't want you snarling at me tomorrow."

"I do *not* snarl," Melanie protested, shooting him a quelling glance as he closed her door and rounded the hood of the car to slide beneath the wheel. She was secretly pleased that he'd remembered she found it difficult to function without eight hours of sleep.

"Besides, I don't need ten hours of sleep, I need eight."

"Hmmmh," Cole grinned at her as he backed out of the parking space, "seems to me it was ten. And, if you don't snarl, at least you have to admit to being cranky."

"I'll admit to cranky," she conceded, "but never grouchy."

He continued to tease her as he drove across town, but by the time he parked in her driveway and walked her up the sidewalk, their efforts to maintain light conversation and ignore the sparks of electrical attraction between them had faded into a taut silence.

Cole unlocked her door, and Melanie stepped over the threshold and turned to face him in a repeat of the previous evening's movements. But this time, when she held out her palm, he dropped the silver key ring into her outstretched hand and reached up to brush a strand of hair from her cheek and tuck it behind her ear.

"Melanie," he said softly, his gaze following the movements of his hand. "I don't want to leave you."

She'd told herself that she would thank him politely and say good night with a handshake. But that was before she heard his voice catch and become a deep, husky murmur when he said her name. That was before she felt the faint tremble in the calloused fingers that smoothed her hair over her shoulder and returned to cup her cheek. That was before he turned his gaze to meet hers and she found the same deep, tormented longing in his blue eyes that ripped at her own heart.

So, with an instinctive response as old as time itself, she stepped naturally into his arms and turned her mouth up to his.

"Melanie," he groaned with heartfelt relief. It was all he had time for before his mouth took hers in a kiss that lacked any preliminary tentativeness. None was needed. The last two hours swaying together on the dance floor had slowly stoked banked fires, until they were both smoldering with explosive heat.

Cole felt the responsive fire ignite Melanie and his arms closed around her, his mouth opening over hers. Her arms tightened around his neck, and she went up on tiptoe, her hips snugging against his. Cole groaned as the notch of her thighs cradled him. He lifted her higher to lock an arm under the curve of her bottom and across the tops of her bare legs, while his tongue surged into her mouth, demanding hers in response as their mouths echoed the hungry straining of his hips against hers.

He tore his mouth from hers to let her breathe, his lips brushing hot, tasting kisses over the fragile, heated skin of her cheeks and the delicate structure of eyelids and lashes.

"Baby," he breathed against the soft skin below her ear, "ask me inside. Let me—please."

Melanie nearly went under at the sensual plea in the husky tones. It promised heaven and blessed relief from the spiraling need that screamed along her nerves.

"Cole," she breathed, closing her eyes against the agony of pleasure that assailed her as his lips moved with warm, hungry insistence against the sensitive skin below her ear. She knew she couldn't allow herself to take the satisfaction he promised and her body craved. "I can't—we can't."

Cole heard the weakened resolve in her throaty protest. Reluctantly, he lifted his head and looked down at her. It was nearly his undoing, for the soft curve of her mouth was faintly swollen and damp from the crush of his, and the green eyes that met his held frustrated passion. She looked willing and wanton. With sudden instinctive sureness, he knew if he picked her up and carried her to her bedroom, she wouldn't protest. But with sudden, clear insight, he realized he wanted more than that.

So, with an effort that cost him dearly, he forced himself to release her.

"You're right," he managed to get out. He bent his head and brushed his mouth against hers for one last time. "I'll call you in the morning."

He stepped back and let the screen door slip closed between them.

"Lock your door," he said huskily, his blue eyes dark with restrained passion. He lifted his hand and laid it palm-up against the screen, and slowly she lifted hers to fit her palm against his.

"Good night," she said softly, and was rewarded by the fleeting smile that crossed his handsome face before she quietly closed the door and turned the deadbolt.

She rested her cheek against the cool wood of the door and listened while his footsteps echoed across the porch and descended the stairs, and until she heard the muted purr of the Thunderbird's engine turn over and fade away down the street.

Melanie, Melanie, what are you doing? She glanced up and saw herself in the hall mirror, and with painful honesty admitted she didn't know if she would have said yes or no if Cole had pushed. *I still want him. Past reason, past pride, in spite of knowing how badly he hurt me last time.*

With a deep sigh, she pushed away from the door and climbed the stairs to her bedroom. Was she going to get through this weekend unscathed and with her heart intact?

Cole was up by eight o'clock the next morning, but he forced himself to wait until the grandfather clock in the hall struck ten before he called Melanie.

"Mmmh, hello." Eyes closed, she fumbled the phone to her ear, her voice an early-morning throaty whisper.

"Good morning, princess," The smile on Cole's face echoed in his voice and carried clearly over the line.

"Good morning," Melanie slitted open one eye and peered at the old-fashioned wind-up alarm clock on her bedside table. "What time is it?"

"Ten o'clock," he said with a grin, picturing her warm and tousled and sleepy. "Time for you to wake up."

"No," she groaned, clutching the phone to her ear and dropping back down on her pillow. "I don't want to."

"Fine," he said agreeably. "I'll come join you and we'll spend the rest of the day in bed. Sounds good to me."

"No!" Eyes wide at last, Melanie sat bolt upright in bed.

"No?" he sounded disappointed, but a deep-throated chuckle carried clearly over the line to her ear. "Too bad. Oh well," he heaved a gusty sigh of regret, "then I guess you'll just have to get up and get dressed before I get over there. Otherwise, I'll join you in bed."

"Don't bother bringing your pajamas," she grumbled sleepily in warning.

"Honey, I don't wear pajamas."

"Oh."

There was dead silence on the line.

"When will you be here?" Melanie cleared her throat and said in a determinedly cheery voice, wishing she could recall that telltale, breathy oh.

"Will a half hour give you enough time to shower and dress?"

"A half hour will be fine," she asserted, grimly assuring herself that she would be dressed and ready or die trying.

"Great! I'll pick you up in thirty minutes."

"Right. Bye," Melanie mumbled in response and dropped the receiver back into its holder before flopping down onto the mattress and staring up at the white ceiling through slitted eyes. "Oooh," she grumbled to herself. "I hate people that are bright-eyed and cheery in the morning!"

Reluctantly, she forced her sluggish body from the bed and staggered into the bathroom.

By the time the doorbell rang precisely thirty minutes later, she'd showered, dressed in casual white slacks and a green cotton top, applied makeup, and was descending the stairs.

She swung the heavy oak door inward and eyed Cole's broad-shouldered body without expression.

Cole grinned at the heavy-eyed look. Clearly, she wasn't awake yet. Some things about Melanie hadn't changed at all. She was still definitely not a morning person. Without a word, he pulled open the screen door and tugged her gently outside, closing the door behind her, and took her arm to walk her down the steps and tuck her into the car.

He slid into the driver's seat and leaned over to pick up a paper bag from the floorboard. Still without speaking, he opened the bag and took out two large travel mugs with lids. He passed one slowly under Melanie's nose and was rewarded by a widening of her thick lashes as she inhaled the aromatic steam from hot black coffee. Her hands reached up and grasped the mug. Cole grinned, propped his elbow on the back of her seat, and leaned his chin on his hand while he watched her sip the black brew.

Melanie drank a quarter of the hot liquid before she sighed softly and relaxed. For the first time, she realized the car hadn't moved—they were still parked in her driveway. She glanced at Cole to find him lounging lazily sideways, his knee propped against the console, watching her with an amused, affectionate expression.

"What are you doing?" she asked in confusion.

"Waiting for you to become conscious," he said with a lopsided grin, "which it seems you just did. Good morning, sunshine," he said softly, and bent forward to brush a kiss against the soft corner of her mouth.

"Good morning." Melanie's reflexes were still too sluggish to object to his kisses. She just couldn't drum up the energy. Besides, it felt wonderful to be sitting enclosed in the car with him so near at hand, smiling at her as if he, too, felt the same warm sense of contentment. "Where are we going today?"

"To a racetrack."

Melanie stopped drinking and stared at him.

"Where?"

"Just across the line in Minnesota," he replied.

"Oh." Melanie was relieved to hear it. For a moment, she'd thought he meant they were flying to Georgia.

He straightened in his seat and handed Melanie the paper bag.

"Here's a little something to go with your coffee," he said as he twisted the key in the ignition and backed out into the street.

Melanie peered into the bag and smiled with blissful delight.

"Maple bars! My favorite!" She shot him a blazing smile that lit her face and her green eyes. "How did you remember?"

"I remember everything about you," he said softly, his gaze flicking from the road to move with quick, hot intensity over her features before his blue eyes went carefully neutral and he smiled, his mouth quirking upward in a heartstopping, friendly grin. "I especially remember how you don't really wake up, but just walk around on automatic pilot until you have a cup of coffee in the morning."

Melanie frowned, trying to remember. She'd certainly never spent the night with him, so how did he know how she woke up in the morning?"

"How do you know that?" she asked suspiciously, wondering if he had her confused with some other green-eyed brunette in the past.

"Because you almost walked off the end of the dock when I picked you up to go fishing early one morning. You were nearly comatose until I poured half a thermos of coffee into you." He flicked another glance over her features. "How did you get hooked on caffeine so young?"

"At school," she responded, absentmindedly sipping her coffee.

"In high school?"

"Yes—don't ask me why they let us have coffee. Heaven knows they had very strict rules about everything else, but for some reason they let us drink tea and coffee."

"Did you go to boarding school all through high school?" he asked, deciding to take advantage of her half-awake state to find out as much as he could about her, and the girl she'd been eight years ago.

"Mm-hmmm," Melanie answered, watching the cornfields whisk by outside the car window, "and junior high, too."

"Must have seemed strange to come back here for the summer after being gone most of the year," he said casually, keeping his gaze on the narrow strip of blacktop ahead of them.

"Yes, it did," Melanie licked maple frosting from her fingertip and munched on the pastry. "After a year or two, I didn't really have any close friends in CastleRock anymore. They'd either moved away or were busy with other friends."

"Sounds lonely," he commented, sipping from the heavy plastic travel mug.

"It was," she agreed, narrowing her eyes at the herd of Jersey cows grazing in the green pasture on their left as they slowed for a stop sign. "It would have helped if I'd had brothers and sisters, but I was an only child so—," she shrugged. "It was probably nothing like your childhood—at least you have brothers, and you have Sarah."

"Yeah," a grin chased across his handsome features as he glanced right, then left, before pulling out onto the highway that would take them north and across the Minnesota state line. "I had brothers all right, who tormented the hell out of me, and I had Sarah, who did the same. There were lots of times when I wished I was an only child."

"Yes, but you weren't," Melanie recognized the affection beneath the wry words, "and I'll bet you wouldn't trade one of them for anything in the world. Come on, admit it, you really like them, don't you?"

"All right, all right," Cole laughed, flicking her an amused glance. "I admit they're not so bad. But if you ever tell a single one of them I said that, I'll deny it."

"I'll have to remember that, in case I ever need to blackmail you," she said impishly, glancing sideways at him through her lashes.

Cole's breath caught in his throat. This was the Melanie he remembered, relaxed and comfortable, affectionate and teasing. Maybe, just maybe, there was hope for them yet.

Unaware of his thoughts, Melanie drank her coffee and happily ate her way through two maple bars as they drove north. By the time they joined the stream of cars entering the gravel parking lot outside the wooden bleachers that marked one side of a paved oval track, she was fully awake.

Cole parked the car under the shade of an oak tree at the edge of the lot and pushed open his door. By the time he'd locked it and walked around the back of the car, Melanie was already out of her seat, her green eyes bright with interest as she watched the streams of spectators wending their way across the parking lot to funnel past the ticket seller and through the gate.

Her hair lay in a heavy curtain across her shoulders, and Cole closed his hand gently over a fistful of the black silk, feeling the heat trapped in its sun-warmed thickness.

"Do you want to take time to put your hair up?" he asked. "It can get damned hot sitting in the bleachers."

"Maybe I should," Melanie turned and bent to rummage in her purse on the car seat. The movement tugged her hair free of his hands. When she turned back to him, he was watching her, hands propped on his hips. She quickly brushed her hair and handed him the brush to hold while she deftly French-braided the long strands from the crown of her head to her nape and tucked the ends under, slipping pins into the bottom to secure it. "There." She took the brush from his hands and dropped it back into her purse. He'd watched her with silent fascination while she tamed the loose mass of black silk into a neat, shiny braid, his eyes never leaving her. "I should just cut it off and be done with it," she said self-consciously.

"No!" his reaction was instant and adamant, and he frowned at her. "Don't ever cut it."

"It would be lots easier to take care of. And besides, long hair is old-fashioned. I've been thinking about getting it cut really, really short—like a bob."

"What the hell is a bob?"

"It's . . ." she began, but he interrupted her.

"Never mind, I don't care what it looks like. Don't cut it."

Silenced, Melanie stared at him. He frowned back at her, his jaw set stubbornly. Part of her wanted to tell him flatly that it was her hair, not his, and that it was none of his business whether she left it long or shaved her head bald. But part of her was secretly pleased he cared whether her hair was short or long.

"Why?" she asked, unable to stifle her need to hear his reason.

"Because you have beautiful hair, and I like it long," his voice lowered and turned raspy, lashes narrowing over blue eyes that turned instantly hot as they met hers. "I still have dreams about how it felt sliding over my skin when we made love."

Melanie gasped, her eyes widening at the instant, clear images evoked by his words.

"You shouldn't say things like that," she managed to get out, her gaze trapped by his, every nerve vividly aware of the tension in his hard body only a few inches from hers.

"Why not? It's true," he said softly, and he reached out to trace the hot color over her cheekbone with his fingertips. "Don't tell me you don't remember, I can tell that you do."

"I remember," Melanie said with painful honesty. "But I don't want to—there's no point in remembering something that's over and done with."

"It doesn't have to be," he murmured, his blue eyes searching hers.

"Yes, it does," she answered, and stepped back, removing herself from the gentle stroking of his fingers against her skin.

He stared at her for a long moment.

"Then we won't remember," he said. "We'll start from here and build new memories."

Melanie stared back at him and shook her head slowly.

"I don't think that's a good idea," she said. "I don't want a scrapbook of memories of a weekend spent with a celebrity. I want a real life, Cole, and that's not something you can give me."

His handsome face was completely expressionless. Then his features softened, and he smiled at her, the blue eyes lighting with warm affection and an emotion she couldn't define, and he reached out to catch her hand in his and tug her toward him.

"Real life, huh?" Cole looked down into her earnest, delicate features and restrained the urge to haul her against him and kiss her breathless. "Are we talking little white houses and picket fences with roses, and church weddings?"

Melanie stiffened and frowned at him.

"No, we are not!"

"No?" His deep voice sounded regretful. "Does that mean you think I'm too much of a lost cause to be considered husband material?"

"I don't consider *anyone* to be husband material. I don't plan to ever get married."

"Why not?" He started walking across the parking lot toward the ticket gate, swinging their clasped hands between them.

"Why should I? I'm perfectly happy as I am. I have a successful business I enjoy, a busy social life, lots of interests. Why should I get married?" She voiced all the reasons she'd repeated to friends and family a thousand times over the last several years. They didn't sound any more convincing now than they had all those other times.

"I have all those things, too, but I still want to get married someday," he answered.

"Why?" she asked curiously.

"Because—the bottom line is—a single life is a lonely life," he glanced sideways at her bent head. "Don't you get lonely, Melanie?"

The words pierced her armor and arrowed straight through her heart.

Yes, her heart cried, *every moment since you left. It never goes away.*

She lifted eyes gone dark with pain to meet his searching blue gaze.

"Cole! Cole McFadden, you son-of-a-gun! What brings you back here?"

SIX

Cole wrenched his gaze away from Melanie's and looked up. They'd paused a few feet from the ticket booth and the little gray-haired ticket seller was leaning out over the counter, a broad smile beaming across her wrinkled face.

"Annie McKinstry! Love of my life!" Cole reached the booth in two strides and, still holding Melanie's hand firmly in his, leaned forward and slid an arm around the elderly woman's round body to hug her. She reached up and gave him a kiss on the cheek and a hug in return, before settling back on her stool to beam at him.

"My goodness, it's good to see you! I don't have to ask you what you've been up to all these years! I watch you racing on television every chance I get." She eyed him proudly. "You've done good, boy."

"Thanks, Annie," Cole grinned at her before looking down at Melanie. "Melanie, this is Annie McKinstry, a diehard racing fan."

"Nice to meet you, Annie," Melanie reached out and had her hand taken in a brief, no-nonsense grip.

"Same here, honey," Annie shrewdly read the possessiveness in Cole's grip on Melanie's hand and the expression in his blue eyes as he looked at her. "You from around here, honey?"

"Yes—I live in CastleRock."

"Ahh, so that's where Cole found you," Annie's sharp glance flicked over Cole's broad figure. "I read in the papers that you were hurt in a crash, but you look healthy."

"That was a month and a half ago, Annie; I broke my leg, but it's nearly good as new."

"Good, good," the gray curls bobbed as she nodded in approval.

"Who's racing today?" Cole asked as he released Melanie's soft hand to pull his billfold from his back pocket and slide a bill across the counter. "Anybody I know?"

"Hmmmm, let me think." Annie took the money and made change from the apron tied around her ample waist. "Charlie Atkins is here, and Kenny Johnson. Oh, yeah, and the Monroe brothers, do you remember them?"

"Sure do," Cole accepted his change from her gnarled fingers and slung an arm across Melanie's shoulders, tucking her against his side. "Sounds as if half the old crew is here. See you later, Annie."

"You bet, Cole, take care. Nice to meet you, honey."

"It was nice to meet you, too, Annie," Melanie said over her shoulder as Cole walked her through the gate and down the grassy alley between the wooden bleachers.

Ahead of them and separating the bleachers from the paved track was a high wire fence. The sounds of the crowd and the powerful car engines were muted by the tunnel they walked through, but the moment they stepped out of the alley, the noise hit them like a living wall of sound. The roar of engines filled the air from the pit area adjacent to the bleachers, and the crowd in the stands added their input to the cacophony when they yelled, whistled, and cheered as the announcer named each car and its driver.

Melanie clapped her hands over her ears and gazed around her in sheer disbelief.

Cole saw the movement and bent to yell in her ear.

"They'll calm down after the announcer finishes introducing the drivers."

Melanie nodded, but didn't reply. She doubted she could have made herself heard over the noise of the crowd and engines, so she merely followed him when he slid his arm from her shoulders, took her hand, and led her up the steps to find a seat. He kept climbing until the crowd thinned out. They were only a few rows from the top before he stopped and waved her ahead of him into an empty row of seats.

She sank onto the wooden bench. Cole had

climbed high enough in the bleachers that the overhang threw its shadow over their seats, giving them blessed relief from the sun's relentless rays beating down from a cloudless, electric blue sky. Melanie inspected the scene spread below them with fascination, while Cole flipped through the program Annie had given him with his change.

"I've watched races on television, but I didn't realize it would be this noisy!" Melanie said, leaning close to shout in Cole's ear so he could hear her over the roar of the crowd.

"They tone it down for TV," his lips brushed her ear as he answered her. "Otherwise, televisions across the United States would probably have their speakers blown out."

Melanie laughed and nodded her head in agreement. She watched the cars circling the track below for several moments until the announcer finished the list of drivers and sponsors. The crowd noise lowered and it was once again possible to carry on a conversation without shouting. "Are they racing already?" Melanie asked, turning to Cole.

"No, they're just running practice laps," Cole explained. "The actual heat races won't start until seven o'clock tonight."

"What's a heat race?" Melanie asked, diverted from the sight of the brightly-painted cars maneuvering for position on the paved track below.

"The elimination races leading up to the main event," Cole said. "The cars finishing in the top five places in each heat race earn the right to run in the main event."

"So, if you don't place in the top five in your first race, you don't get a chance to race anymore?"

"That's right," Cole said, "you load it on the trailer and go home."

"Oh," Melanie was silent for a moment as she watched the cars driving around the oval below. "That must be incredibly disappointing."

"Yeah," Cole drawled. "You're all dressed-up with no place to go."

"Why are they driving around the track now, if the real races don't start till tonight?"

"Testing the car, testing the track." At Melanie's uncomprehending look, Cole gestured to the track below and explained. "To win a race, you don't just have to have a car that's fast, you have to have a car that's set up just right for the track and the weather. If it's been raining, the track surface is going to be slick as ice when the water combines with the oil on the pavement. If it's hot and dry, you can still have a problem if there's oil on the track. And the barometric pressure determines if the car's running rich or lean."

Melanie had been listening intently, but she shook her head in confusion and lifted a hand to interrupt him.

"Wait—I'm confused. What do you mean, you don't just need a fast car to win the race? I thought speed was what a race was all about."

"A fast car is important, but races are won or lost in the turns. It's how a car handles, not how fast it is that ultimately determines if it's a winner." Cole's gaze flicked from Melanie's delicate features to the cars circling the track below. "There's a perfect example," he drew her attention to the track. "See number forty-eight—the red Chevrolet with *Pettigrew Muffler Shop* printed in black letters across the side?"

Melanie followed his pointing finger and found the car he was describing.

"Yes, I see it."

"Watch it go through the turns—it's pushing. That means it's under steering—the front end doesn't want to turn. The force compelling it to go in a straight line is fighting the force turning it into the curve. See how it slows and falls slightly behind the Oldsmobile, number seventeen, in the turns, then he catches him on the straightaway. The Chevy is faster, but seventeen handles better in the turns."

"So, how do you fix that?" Melanie's attention was fastened on the track, watching as the two cars proved the truth of Cole's observations, as the Chevy consistently caught the Oldsmobile on the straightaways and fell slightly behind in the turns.

"The Chevy needs more wedge in the chassis, and you can do that in a number of ways." Caught up in his explanation, he glanced at Melanie to find her frowning at him. Before she could stop him again, he laughed and explained, "Wedging a chassis is lifting it higher on one side so it corners better. Sometimes it can be done with tire stagger—that means varying the actual height of the tires to lift one side higher."

"My goodness," Melanie stared at him with an

arrested expression. "It's not exactly like driving the family sedan, is it?"

"Nope," Cole grinned at her. "Most people think that you just get in a car with a big engine and drive it as fast as you can around and around in a circle, and whoever finishes the most laps first, wins. There's a lot more to it."

"You love it, don't you?" Melanie asked, seeing the warm gleam in his eyes and the intent absorption on his hard features.

"Yeah," he glanced down at her, smiling self-consciously. "It shows, huh?"

"Yes." Her heart swelled with a surge of warm affection for the boy inside the hard man, and his passionate devotion to his work. She clasped her hands tightly together on her knees to keep from obeying the overwhelming urge to brush his hair back off his brow and smooth her palm over the thick, tawny strands. Instead, she smiled back at him, unaware that her expression reflected the affectionate warmth that filled her. "If you're trying to hide it, Mr. McFadden, it's not working," she teased.

Cole looked down into her face and was gripped with an emotion that scared the hell out of him. Her green eyes were soft, her face alight with teasing mischief and relaxed warmth as she tilted her face up to his. He felt disoriented, and the years fell away as he was suddenly twenty-five again and madly, head-over-in-heels in love with her.

Oh no, he groaned silently, unable to rip his gaze away from her. *This can't be happening. All I really wanted was a chance to take her to bed and exorcise her memory!* But his heart didn't listen, and in the back of his mind, a tiny voice laughed quietly, deriding him for refusing to face the truth. *Sure you did,* the little voice chortled. *That's why you spent ten thousand dollars just to guarantee forty-eight hours of her company! You could have taken her to bed the other night if all you wanted was her body!*

"Cole?"

Melanie's voice interrupted him and he snapped back to awareness to find her looking at him with a tiny, worried frown pulling down her brows.

"Is something wrong?"

"No—no, nothing's wrong," he said abruptly. *Not unless you consider the fact that I'm probably about to make a complete fool of myself. Again,* he thought bleakly.

"So," he said with forced cheerfulness, "where were we?"

"You were telling me how much you love racing," Melanie replied.

"Oh, yeah. Boring subject," Cole said. "What else do you want to know about racing itself?"

The sun climbed higher and began its journey toward the west, while Cole explained the point system that determined a driver's placement in the competition for the season championship. He answered Melanie's questions with unfailing patience, secretly delighted at her interest and her obvious fascination with the details of stock car racing and the rush toward the finals unfolding on the track below.

They left the track at four o'clock and drove into

the small farming community to have dinner at a cafe, where mouth-watering steaks more than made up for the restaurant's plain decor and oilcloth-covered tables.

They were back at the track and seated in the bleachers well before the first heat lap started at seven p.m., Melanie just as eager as Cole for the races to begin.

"Why didn't you tell me watching stock car racing was so much fun?" she asked several hours later, her voice roughened from yelling and cheering by the time the main event ended at eleven o'clock.

"Darned if I know," Cole shrugged, grinning down at her animated face. "Want to go down to the pits and congratulate Charlie?"

"Can we do that?" she asked. "Don't you have to have a pass, or something?"

"Usually, but Charlie's a friend of mine. I'm sure they'll let us in." He didn't add that his own name would gain him instant entry to the pit area at any stock car track in the United States. "Come on." He took her hand and drew her to her feet. They wound their way through the crowd exiting the stadium and around to the far side of the track, where they were halted by a wire gate and a guard in T-shirt and jeans.

"Sorry, Mac," the burly guard said, "but spectators aren't allowed past the fence and into the pits."

"I'm a friend of Charlie Atkins," Cole answered easily. "He'll vouch for me."

"Sure," the guard said skeptically, his weary tone

clearly reflecting that he'd heard that line before. "What's your name, and I'll tell him you're here."

"Cole McFadden."

"McFadden?" The guard did a doubletake, his jaded look sharpening as it ran over the man on the other side of the gate. His eyes widened and a broad smile spread across his face. "Well, hell, Mr. McFadden, I reckon I don't have to check with Charlie. Come on in."

"Thanks," Cole's hand moved to Melanie's waist and he urged her gently ahead of him through the open gate. "Where is Charlie?"

"Just down the line there, sixth from the end," the burly man gestured with a big paw to the row of cars, trailers, equipment, and crew members.

"Thanks," Cole said.

"My pleasure," the man held out his hand and shook Cole's enthusiastically. "I'm a big fan of yours, Mr. McFadden. I was sure sorry to hear about your crash and I'm glad to see you're lookin' healthy. Are you gonna be back racing soon?"

"Hard to say—the doctors tell me not for another six weeks or so," Cole answered easily.

"Six weeks? That's too bad; Conoley will probably knock you out of the points race by then, won't he?"

"Most likely," Cole agreed, his broad shoulders lifted in a shrug of indifference. "But that's racing—you win some, you lose some. Thanks for letting us in."

"Hey, no problem. Anytime." The guard grinned

and lifted a hand in good-bye as Cole drew Melanie away.

Cole's voice had held a philosophical acceptance of his ill luck, which surprised her, and Melanie glanced up at him, trying to read his face. "Aren't you upset that the accident caused you to lose so much time away from racing this summer?"

"I can't say that I'm happy about it," Cole turned his head and looked down at her. "It knocks me out of the point standings for the championship this year. But on the other hand," he slung an arm across her shoulders and slowed his stride, "if I hadn't been injured, I wouldn't have come back to CastleRock. And I would have missed this weekend with you. All things considered, I can't say I'm sorry about any of it."

Melanie's steps slowed to keep pace with his and she stared up at him. Beneath the pit area's bright lights, his eyes gleamed deeply blue between their thick fringe of dark blond lashes. She tried to gauge the depth of his sincerity, but her insecurity and lack of trust in her own judgment made it impossible for her to know if he meant what he said, or if he was only repeating a line he used with all the women he dated. She looked away from him and found they were nearly opposite the blue Chevy painted with the number seventy-two.

"We're here," she said, pointing at the car. "Isn't that the car that belongs to Charlie Atkins?"

Cole glanced up, his gaze following her finger.

"Yup, that's Charlie's Chevy, all right." Keeping Melanie tucked close against his side, he walked up to the nearest crew member and tapped him on the shoulder. "Excuse me, is Charlie around?"

The young man barely looked at Cole and continued packing tools into a metal case. "Yeah, he's on the other side of the car—standing by the van with his wife."

"Thanks." Cole steered Melanie around the hood of the stock car. Before they'd gone three steps toward the van and the group of people who stood or leaned against the silver paint, a bellow of surprise greeted them.

"Cole McFadden!"

The half-circle of people moved apart, a chorus of delighted greetings accompanying the grins of recognition that spread across male and female faces alike. A burly, bearded, middle-aged man shouldered his way through the group. "I'll be damned! It is you!" Charlie Atkins grinned from ear to ear, his smile a white slash in the black beard that covered the lower half of his face. He covered the space between them and swept Cole into a bone-crushing hug.

Melanie moved out from under Cole's arm just in time to escape being included in the greeting. She winced as Charlie stepped back and shook Cole's hand, giving him a hearty slap on the shoulders that would have staggered a lesser man. *What is it with men?* she thought with bewilderment. *Can't they just say hello without bombarding each other?*

"How you been, boy?"

"Fine, just fine," Cole grinned at his old mentor. Charlie Atkins had been racing at the small Minnesota track for as long as Cole could remember. He'd never raced nationally, but he was a local legend long before Cole was old enough to apply for his first driver's license. He'd watched Cole drive in his first race and taken him under his wing, gruffly telling him that if he didn't kill himself first, he'd be driving at Daytona someday.

"I hear you ran a car into a wall and smashed up your leg," Charlie said, sweeping a keen searching look over Cole from head to toe. "You don't look much the worse for wear."

"I'm mending," Cole said noncommittally. "You know how it is, Charlie, the papers always make everything a lot worse than it is."

"Mmhh," Charlie grunted in acknowledgment at the truth of the statement and his acceptance of Cole's unwillingness to discuss his injury. His gaze left Cole, and for the first time he noticed Melanie. "And who is this?" he said with unabashed interest.

Cole reached out and caught Melanie's hand, his fingers threading through hers as he drew her near. "This is Melanie Winters—and she's mine, so keep your hands off, you old reprobate." The laughter underlying the threat took the sting from his words.

"Hell, I'm married, boy!" Charlie pretended to look insulted, but the brown eyes that fixed approvingly on Melanie snapped with amusement. "But she sure is pretty enough to tempt a man. Nice to meet you, Melanie."

"It's nice to meet you, too, Charlie. I enjoyed watching you race—congratulations on winning."

"Thanks," Charlie said expansively, grinning

broadly. "It's always better to win than to lose, right, Cole?"

"No contest," Cole said drily.

"Hey, I want you to meet my wife," Charlie said and caught Cole's elbow in one hand to tug him forward to join the group standing next to the van. "Sandy, this is Cole McFadden. You remember, I told you I used to race with him."

"That's an understatement," Cole smiled at the blonde as he shook her hand. "It's probably more accurate to say that he *taught* me to race with him."

"Oh, hell," Charlie's face, the small part that was visible between his beard and the bill of his baseball cap, turned red with embarrassment, but he beamed with pleasure. "I wouldn't go that far."

"He's modest," Sandy said with a smile of affection at her husband, "but he's told me lots of stories about the two of you, and the Monroe brothers—when you all raced together."

"Uh-oh," Cole laughed, shooting a threatening look at Charlie. "I hope he didn't tell you everything we did."

"Nah," Charlie denied, "not everything. We still might get arrested, even after all these years."

Cole chuckled and tucked Melanie closer against his side, glancing down at her with warm green eyes. "This is Melanie Winters, Sandy, and I *haven't* told her any incriminating stories, so don't repeat any of the wilder stuff Charlie told you."

"Nice to meet you, Melanie," Sandy said, taking her hand in a brief, friendly grip. "We'll have to get together and compare stories about these two."

"Now, there's an idea," Charlie said. "We're all going down to Donovan's Tavern to celebrate our win. You and Melanie come with us—it'll give us a chance to swap war stories and let the women compare all the lies we've been tellin' them."

"How about it, Melanie?" Cole looked down at her, trying to gauge her reaction to the suggestion.

Melanie glanced around the semicircle of faces and found only friendly welcome. These were Cole's friends, they'd known him since long before she met him that fateful summer, and she felt a swift surge of intense desire to satisfy her curiosity about his life. Her weekend with him was nearly over, their time was running out, and she might never have another chance to learn more about him.

"It sounds like fun," she answered, smiling up into his eyes.

Cole felt a surge of pride. She'd been a good sport about the whole weekend. With her innate sense of style, unconsciously proud carriage, and her background of private school and wealthy parents, she was clearly out of her element among the good-old-boy drivers and their wives, but she seemed oblivious to the differences.

"All right," he turned back to Charlie, "count us in. I'll buy the first round."

The crowd let out whoops of approval and began to break up, heading for their vehicles.

"We'll meet you at Donovan's, Charlie," Cole said.

"Great—we're almost through packing up the

equipment. Give us another half hour or so—save us a table.''

''Right.'' Cole walked back the way they'd come, exiting through the gate. With Melanie tucked against his side and his arm across her shoulders, their hips bumped as they strolled back to the parking lot, the contact a sweet torture he couldn't bring himself to break. ''Are you sure you want to go to Donovan's, Melanie?'' he looked down at her. ''We don't have to if you don't want to.''

''No, it's fine,'' she smiled up at him, the bright lights illuminating her face, her lashes throwing mysterious shadows across her green eyes. ''Besides, I want to hear the stories about the good old days and all the wild things you did.''

Cole groaned and shook his head.

''I knew this was a bad idea!''

Donovan's Tavern was packed with race crews and fans. Cigarette smoke drifted in a blue cloud and mixed with the heat generated by the sheer number of bodies crowded in the wooden structure. Country music blared from a jukebox in the corner to compete with the noise of people talking and the frequent bursts of laughter.

Melanie and Sandy returned from a trip to the ladies room to find their chairs taken, and four more people crowded around the round table.

''Here, honey,'' Charlie slung an arm around Sandy's waist and pulled her down onto his lap, continuing his story with hardly a pause.

Melanie stood next to Cole, her hand resting on

his shoulder while she listened to the burst of laughter that greeted the punchline of Charlie's joke. Cole's fingers closed over hers and tugged her closer. She bent her head, trying to ignore the shivers that feathered over her skin when his lips brushed her ear while he spoke.

"Do you want to leave?" he asked.

She turned her head and looked into his eyes, thick-lashed eyes so close she could see the little flecks of cobalt in the blue irises.

"No," she said. "Not yet."

"Then sit down," he said, his voice rasping huskily.

Melanie glanced around the crowded table. "Where?"

"Here."

Her gaze raced back to his, and found him watching her with an intentness that was disconcerting.

Cole smiled at the uncertainty in the green eyes that met his, and tugged her forward before he caught her waist in his hands and pulled her off balance and onto his lap.

Startled, Melanie perched stiffly sideways on his knees, finding it impossible to relax even when Cole slid his arms around her waist and eased her back until her shoulder touched his chest. After a few moments, when he didn't hug her closer or move his hands from where they rested against her waist and hip, she chanced a sideways glance at him from beneath the concealing fringe of her lashes. He wasn't paying any attention to her. Instead, he was listening to Charlie tell another story. Melanie let out a deep breath and imperceptibly relaxed a fraction of an inch.

Don't be such a ninny, she chided herself. *He's only being polite—there isn't anywhere else to sit.* Her muscles loosened a tiny fraction more and her attention shifted to Charlie.

"And then there was the time we drove all the way to Bakersfield for the drags, remember, Cole?"

"Oh, geez," Cole groaned, "do I ever."

"Do you mean Bakersfield, California?" Melanie asked disbelievingly.

"Yup, sure do—halfway across the United States just so Cole could watch Don Prudhomme drive," Charlie paused to tip an amber bottle of beer up for a long swig. He wiped the back of his hand across his mouth and eyed Cole with disgust. "Eighteen hours in that damn van—and when we got to Bakersfield, it was the middle of the night and there wasn't a vacant motel room in town. Everybody on the west coast must have shown up for those races!"

"What are you complaining about, Charlie? You wound up with a free room for the night," Cole said without heat, only half-listening to his friend. He was paying much more attention to the woman he held in his arms. Melanie was listening to Charlie, her face animated as she focused on his words, the soft curve of her bottom snuggling into Cole's lap as her body unconsciously adjusted to fit against his. Cole tucked her shoulder more comfortably under his and tightened his hold on her hip, his fingers splaying lower over the top of her thigh.

"Yeah—in jail!" Charlie complained. Encouraged

by Melanie's expression of rapt attention, he waved the amber bottle to include the dozen listeners at the table. Charlie loved to tell stories, and he was in his element with his audience hanging on every word. "The kid, here, decided he was hungry, starving, and insisted we find a place to eat. Well, hell, the only place open at two in the morning in Bakersfield, California, was a godforsaken, rundown, all-night diner. But he insists, so we go in and sit down at the counter. The place was none too clean, but we ordered anyway and the food wasn't half bad. We're sitting there, eating and minding our own business, and in comes six or seven bikers—I mean, *real* bikers! They were all about seven-feet tall and just as wide, and they all wore black leather with chains everywhere. And mean lookin'! Geez, nobody with any brains would have said boo to those guys."

"I didn't say boo to them, Charlie," Cole protested mildly, a small smile curving his mouth.

"It would have been better if you did!"

"What did he do?" Melanie asked, absentmindedly resting her arm and hand over Cole's.

"The damn fool laughed at them!" Charlie said with a disgusted snort.

"Why?"

"Tell her why, Charlie," Cole interjected, trying to control the heat that was slowly pounding through his veins.

"Bugs," Charlie said succinctly, and paused dramatically, his brown gaze moving around the circle of expectant faces, a grin splitting his black beard as their expressions reflected confusion. "Yup, bugs.

The bikers sat down at the counter, and the one that sat next to me was a huge bear of a man, with greasy black hair in a ponytail and the thickest, bushiest beard I'd ever seen . . ."

"Thicker than yours, Charlie?" Sandy interrupted, and laughed when he growled threateningly at her.

"Quiet, woman. This guy had hair all over his face, and it was chockful of bugs. Not just a couple of mosquitoes, mind you, but bugs! Big ones, little ones. I mean to tell you, his beard and hair looked like the bug screen on a cross-country semi! And Cole points the bugs out to me in a whisper that could have been heard from Bakersfield to L.A.! Fortunately, the big guy didn't hear him. But then the biker ordered soup, and I don't know if he was drunk or just plain tired, but he slurped that soup slower and slower. Until finally, he went to sleep in it!" He nodded at Melanie's widened, disbelieving eyes. "Yup, it's true. He just fell face forward into his soup bowl and started snoring. And then Cole, polite youngster that he was, busted up laughing."

"And the guy in the soup got mad?" Melanie asked.

"No—he just kept sleeping, snoring away in his soup. But his friends took offense and decided to teach us some manners. By the time the owner called the cops and they got there, the diner was a wreck and the police carted us all off to jail." Charlie shook his head and took a swig of his beer. "Hell of a way to see California," he said musingly.

"Did you miss seeing the races?" Melanie asked.

"Nah, we bailed out of jail the next morning and Cole got to see Prudhomme drive, after all."

Melanie, convulsed with laughter, turned a mirthful face up to Cole. The wry blue glance that met hers held amusement and an underlying flicker of blue flame. Her smile faded and she became instantly aware of his hard body. The banked fire that lay deep in his eyes matched the warmth simmering in her own veins.

Cole watched the green eyes heat with longing and an answering awareness that matched the desire that tormented his own body with nearly unbearable sexual tension. His heart lurched at the undisguised need written on her face and his muscles tensed, waiting for her to deny it and distance herself from him. But her gaze didn't drop from his. Instead of tensing and shifting away from him, her body softened and imperceptibly molded closer to his.

With an abruptness that startled Melanie and had her clutching his arm for balance, he picked her up and stood her on her feet. He pushed out of the chair with one smooth movement and tucked her under his arm, flashing an apologetic grin at Charlie.

"Sorry, Charlie, but it's getting late and I promised Melanie I'd get her home early. So, we have to take off."

"So soon? But it's early . . ."

"I know, but we have to drive back to CastleRock."

Charlie shook Cole's outstretched hand, and Melanie barely had time to answer a chorus of good-byes from the group at the table before Cole was moving quickly through the crowded tavern.

He didn't speak as they crossed the parking lot, nor when he dug in his pocket for car keys to unlock the passenger door. He handed Melanie inside and followed her.

Melanie scooted to the edge of the bucket seat and watched in confusion as he slid onto the seat beside her and slammed the door.

"What are you . . ." she barely got the words out before he wrapped his arms around her and pulled her onto his lap, his mouth finding hers with unerring precision.

Melanie didn't even consider fighting him. She slid her free arm around his neck and held on as passion exploded between them.

Long, hot moments passed as mouth moved with demanding, tortured need against mouth. Melanie murmured in protest when his lips lifted a fraction of an inch from hers.

"Open your mouth," he demanded in a nearly unintelligible growl. When she obeyed, his hands cradled her head to hold her still while his tongue surged into the sleek wetness. The groan that lifted his chest against her breasts was echoed by the frantic little moans forming in the back of her throat.

Cole's hands moved restlessly over her back and waist before smoothing down the outer curve of her thigh and up again to cup her breast in a possessive, claiming gesture. He was rewarded by a gasp of pleasured shock as Melanie first went still, then twisted to push frantically against his palm. His thumb brushed over the tip of her breast and she moaned beneath his mouth, her fingers flexing against his nape, where her fingernails left little half-moons of torment against his skin.

He nearly tore the buttons off her blouse in his drive to get her bare. She didn't protest when his mouth left hers and trailed hot fire down the soft underside of her jaw and throat to press fiery, open-mouthed kisses against the soft curve of her breast swelling above the low lace of her bra. But when his mouth closed over the cream satin and lace covering the crest, her whole body clenched and arched against his.

Her whimpers of pleasure and frustration echoed in the heated enclosure of the car, and Cole nearly came apart. He pressed his flushed face against the soft swell of her breast and dragged air scented with her perfume and the sweet smell of woman into his lungs, his arms closing almost painfully around her.

"I want you," he breathed harshly, lifting his face. His hand closed over her hair, his fingers tangled in the loosened woven braid, and he tugged her face up to his. His eyes were fiercely demanding, and hot with need and barely-controlled desire. "I want to take you to bed and bury myself in you, until neither of us knows where one begins and the other ends. I want hours and hours of making love to you until we're both exhausted."

SEVEN

A flood of raw desire raced through Melanie's veins at the blatantly sexual picture his words created. Barely inches from hers, his face was flushed with heat, his skin stretched tautly over the hard thrust of his cheekbones and the line of his jaw. Beneath tawny brows, his eyes were heavy-lidded and burning with arousal, and they held promises of pleasures that she ached to taste again. The warm weight of his hand cupped her breast in a possessive, claiming gesture and generated a hot, aching lethargy. It weighted her limbs and destroyed her ability to think beyond the frantic beat of her heart and the heated rush of blood through her veins.

"I want you, too," she admitted in a husky murmur.

Fierce joy leapt in the hot-blue gaze that held hers,

and he bent to claim her lips again. But before he could take her mouth with his, she stopped him with her fingertips against his lips.

"What's wrong?" he rasped.

Melanie's heart shuddered at the feel of his lips moving against the sensitive skin of her fingertips, but she forced herself not to give in to the nearly overwhelming demands of her body.

"I can't just go to bed with you, Cole," she said shakily. "I don't sleep around. Saying yes to you isn't something I can do lightly. And after all, this is only our second date. Wanting you doesn't mean I can go to bed with you."

Cole waged a valiant struggle to conquer his raging hormones, groaning with the effort as he squeezed his eyes shut and rested his forehead against hers.

"All right, honey," he said reluctantly, gathering her against him to press her tightly against the taut muscles of his body, while he buried his face in the scented curve where her throat met the delicate bones of her shoulder. "Maybe I am rushing you. I'm not sure how long I can last, but I'll try like hell to give you time to get used to the idea. But you have to promise to see me and give this relationship a chance."

Shocked, Melanie stiffened and wedged a space between them.

Relationship? The word hinted at growth and permanence. He was the only man who had ever made her forget her morals and principles, the only one to reach beyond the cool wall she erected around her heart and touch the person she was inside. She was ready to admit she wanted him physically, but a *relationship*? The very word terrified her. He'd made promises of forever once before. She'd believed him and it had nearly destroyed her. She couldn't bring herself to walk off the edge of that particular cliff again.

Reluctantly, Cole let her shift a fraction away from him, his head lifting so he could search her expression. Wide green eyes watched him, worry vying with passion in the darkened gaze that met his.

"What?" he murmured gently, one hand lifting to stroke her cheek. "Tell me what put that worried look in those beautiful eyes."

"I'm ready to admit that I want you, Cole," she said softly, her fingers moving to cup his against her cheek when his hand tensed with pleasure at her words. "But that word—*relationship*—sounds so permanent." His eyes narrowed over her face; her voice faltered before she forced herself to continue. "We both know that you'll only be around for a few more weeks, and what we have during this brief time is all there is for us. You'll go back to the east coast and I'll stay here in the midwest—we'll return to our separate lives after your leg has healed. I don't want to pretend there is anymore to this than there is right now, this moment. And I don't want any regrets when you leave—I don't want to get hurt."

Cole heard the tremor in her husky whisper and saw the anxiety lurking below the painful honesty in the gaze that met his without flinching. It was a shock to hear she assumed that he wasn't contemplating anything permanent. He stared at her with unblinking concentration for several long seconds.

"Cole?" she ventured tentatively, his continued silence stirring more misgivings.

"Sorry, honey," his long lashes flicked down and then up. The stillness that had frozen his expression into watchfulness melted, the hard line of his mouth softening, his lower lip curving in a sensual smile that shortened her breath and sent her blood surging through her veins. "I have to admit you've surprised me."

"I know," Melanie admitted, "but I can't deny the way you make me feel. You were right, we strike sparks off each other—"

"Forest fires," he interjected softly.

"Forest fires," she agreed, her cheeks flushing hotter, "and after all, we're both adults, we're not children. If we decide to become more—involved—surely it's no one's business but our own?"

"Absolutely," he said solemnly. Cole was having trouble accepting that the Melanie he'd known before and the Melanie he'd glimpsed over the last two days was the same woman lying in his arms. "So, how much time do you want before I can spend the night?"

Melanie's instant, affronted reaction was to slap him. But he caught her fingers and laughed softly, hugging her against him and covering her face with kisses before his mouth settled over hers, the warm seductive pressure of his lips quickly replacing her indignation with rising passion.

"I guess that means not tonight, huh?" he asked huskily when he finally lifted his head.

"No, not tonight," she answered, her own voice throaty and slurred with pleasure.

"How long?" The restless movements of his hands over her back echoed the restrained urgency in his raspy murmur.

"I don't know," she watched him helplessly, smoothing her fingers over the curve of his cheek and jaw, before trailing an exploring fingertip over the whorls of his ear. "Can't we just see each other and get reacquainted for awhile before we decide if we . . ." she broke off, unable to go on, her lashes falling to hide her eyes from his unfathomable gaze. "I sound ridiculous, don't I? Women have affairs everyday—I don't know why I have to make this so difficult."

"What other women do or don't do has nothing to do with you," he said reassuringly, touched by the honesty she offered him. *Besides*, he thought as he scanned her worried face and searched the darkened green eyes, *you're scared to death to sleep with me. Not of making love, but of the risk of becoming involved.* "Getting reacquainted sounds like a good idea to me, too. So, whenever you're ready to take this any further, let me know. I can stand waiting," a small, wry smile quirked his lips, "just barely—as long as I know you'll stop fighting this attraction we feel for each other, and you won't refuse to see me."

"I won't refuse to see you," she promised, relieved he hadn't made fun of her lack of sophistication.

"Good," his eyes darkened, lashes lowering as his gaze slid caressingly over her face before fastening with single-minded absorption on her mouth. "Now, kiss me again before I take you home and leave you at your door like a good boy."

More than willing, Melanie slid her fingers into the thick hair at his nape and lifted her lips to his, rewarded by his groan of pleasure when her mouth opened beneath his.

After Cole drove her home, the memory of that kiss and the conversation preceding it kept Melanie tossing and turning half the night. The restlessness that tormented her was made worse by the knowledge that it was created only partly by her worry over whether she should have an affair with Cole. The other factor was the unsatisfied hunger for him that tortured her.

"Where is she?"

The irate voice carried clearly through the office wall in the back of Victoria's Garden. Melanie pushed her chair back and slipped reading glasses from her nose to drop them on top of the bookkeeping ledgers lying open atop the desk. She was halfway to the door when it burst open.

"There you are!" he stormed through the doorway, waving a copy of the *CastleRock Independent* he held clenched in his hand. "Are you out of your mind?"

"For heaven's sake, Daddy, what's wrong?" Melanie had never seen her father this angry, his face was flushed, his green eyes glittering with fury.

"I'll tell you what's wrong!" he shouted, and threw the paper down on her desk. It fell open, and there, in five-by-seven-inch grainy black-and-white, was a photo of Cole with his hand at Melanie's waist, leading her from the stage. The caption below was explicit: RACE CAR DRIVER BUYS LOCAL BUSINESSWOMAN AT AUCTION. "*That's* what's wrong!"

"Oh, no," Melanie groaned, closing her eyes to shut out the photo.

"Is that all you have to say?" John Winters demanded, glaring at her with barely restrained fury.

"Daddy, please," Melanie moved quickly to shut the office door, leaning against it for support as she faced her father. "Everyone in the shop can hear you!"

"What difference does it make?" he demanded, but he made a conscious effort to lower his voice. "All anyone in town has to do is pick up the newspaper and there you are, splashed all over the front page!"

"I'm sorry if it embarrasses you—" she began, but her father cut her off in mid-sentence.

"I don't give a damn about that. Nothing you could do would embarrass me. You're my daughter and I love you," John thrust his fingers through his short, regulation-cut hair, the ebony strands that were duplicates of his daughter's mingling with silvery threads. "What I want to know is—what the hell are you doing talking to that man, let alone allowing him to *buy you* at some auction!"

"It was a fund-raiser, Daddy, and I certainly didn't plan to be bought." She pushed away from the door and crossed the tiny office to her desk, leaning one hip on the wooden edge while she stared down at the photo. With sudden clarity, she remembered flinching at the bright flashes of light when she and Cole left the stage and realized that they must have been caused by photographer's flashbulbs.

"Then how did it happen?" he demanded, tugging loose the knot in his tie with a frustrated gesture.

When Melanie explained, he stared at her in disbelief.

"Are you telling me that McFadden gave ten thousand dollars to the Children's Fund just to spend the weekend with you?"

"Yes," Melanie said, bracing for his next question.

"But you didn't actually spend the weekend with him, did you?"

"Yes, Daddy," she said levelly. " I did."

John Winters was speechless.

"You mean, you actually did it?" he said, when he could speak. "You actually spent time with that man?"

"I gave my word, Daddy," she said with quiet determination, "and you're the one who taught me to honor my commitments always."

"Yes, but this—" Her father stared at her for a long, considering moment. "Are you all right? Did he do anything to—"

"No, Daddy, he was a perfect gentleman," Melanie smiled at the relief that smoothed the lines in her father's face, "and I'm fine."

"Well, I suppose there's no damage done, then. He'll leave town soon enough—the weekend is over and done with and it's not as if you'll be seeing him again," he sighed and turned away, but something in her expression stopped him and he turned back to face her. Hands propped on hips, he stared at her consideringly. "You aren't seeing him again," he said slowly, "are you?"

"Yes, Daddy, I am."

"Dammit," he threw his hands up in the air and paced the short confines of her office in agitation. "I can't believe I'm hearing this! Have you forgotten what happened the last time you got involved with him?"

"No, Daddy, I haven't forgotten," Melanie replied with as much calm as she could muster. She folded her arms across her midriff and waited patiently while he paced and muttered.

"Then you must realize that he'll leave again! His life is on the east coast, driving race cars and dating beauty queens! Oh, sure, he'll take you out and spin you a line while he's in town, to pass the time until he's well again. But then he'll be gone—and you'll be left behind to pick up the pieces, just like before!"

"I know all that," Melanie said. "You aren't telling me anything I haven't already told myself."

"Then why in God's name are you leaving yourself open to more heartbreak?" he asked.

Because he makes me feel alive! she thought. *Because I fell in love with him when I was only seventeen and I've just discovered that I never got over him.* But she couldn't tell her father that. It was difficult enough admitting to herself how she felt about Cole. She couldn't say the words out loud.

"I'm not a child anymore," she said instead, meeting his baffled gaze with calm, determined green eyes. "If I want to take chances with a man, I'm old enough to handle it."

"Even if that man is Cole McFadden?" her father shot back.

"Yes," she nodded, "especially if that man is Cole."

"Damn," her father shook his head in frustration and reluctant concession. "I think you're wrong, honey, but you're not seventeen anymore. I guess you're old enough to make your own decisions."

"I haven't done so badly so far, have I?" Melanie said with a wobbly smile, glancing around the little office.

"Not in business, honey," her father said, "but when it comes to McFadden—I don't know. I just don't want to see you get hurt when he leaves again."

"I know he'll leave CastleRock, and I know I might be hurt by his leaving. But I'm a big girl now, and I don't have any illusions about happily-ever-afters."

Dismayed, John Winters didn't know what to say to his daughter. So, he did what fathers the world over have done when confronted with their little girl's adulthood: He gathered her into his arms and hugged her tightly. And silently swore to kill Cole McFadden if he caused even one tear to well in her green eyes.

Melanie saw Cole nightly for the next two weeks. He courted her in every way he knew how—sending her flowers, taking her to dinner, surprising her with small gifts that made her laugh or touched her by their thoughtfulness. She was very careful to see him only in public places, where they would be surrounded by other people. He never voiced an objection, although she knew he must be aware she was avoiding being alone with him and the intimacy she was afraid would surely occur.

After fourteen days and long nights, Cole was beginning to wonder if he could keep his promise to wait to make love with her until she was ready. He found himself constantly reining in his emotions, and his body was in such a state of slowly simmering, permanent arousal that it was driving him crazy.

Just when Cole was questioning his ability to get through another evening ending with a cold shower, and Melanie was wondering if she was ever going to be able to get past her hesitancy and fears and cross the line from "yes" to "now," Angela Winters unwittingly resolved the issue.

Her mother's invitation to lunch in mid-week wasn't unusual, but there had been something in Angela Winters' voice when she telephoned that morning that struck Melanie as strange. Driving the short distance from Victoria's Garden to her parents' lakeside home, Melanie tried to pinpoint exactly what had been different about her mother's voice, but couldn't quite put her finger on it.

She parked beneath the carport, but instead of joining her mother inside, she walked impulsively around the back of the house and followed the path down the slope of mowed lawn past the flowerbeds to the lake. The silvered, worn wooden dock was the same T-shaped structure where she'd first met Cole. She walked slowly to the end of the dock, her heels echoing hollowly against the wooden planks. The green lake waters slapped softly, rhythmically against the wooden pilings. The sun beat down from a cloudless blue sky, and out on the lake boats pulled water skiers in their wakes, while slower fishing skiffs lazily lifted and fell on their waves.

Memories swamped her, stirred by the scent of lakewater and the heated tar on the dock pilings, and by the familiar scene of the summer sun glittering off the surface of the lake. She stared at the end of the dock, remembering Cole's laughing face, his eyes a startling blue against the teak tan of his face.

"Melanie!" Her mother's voice startled her from her reverie, and with an effort, she pulled her thoughts back to the present and turned to climb the slope to the house.

"Hello, Mom," she called as she neared the deck where her mother stood, leaning against the wide railing and watching her approach.

"Hi, honey," Angela replied. "What were you doing down at the dock?"

"Oh, nothing." Melanie climbed the short flight of steps leading to the wooden deck and smiled reassuringly at her mother's curious look. At sixty, Angela Winters hardly looked her age. Her thick black hair was only faintly traced with silver, her blue eyes alert and wise in a face where a minimum of lines testified to her years. In white shorts and sandals, a blue cotton shirt tucked in at the waist, her figure was youthful and athletic. Melanie gave her a quick, affectionate hug that was returned with the same warmth, and she glanced over her mother's shoulder at a round table set with china and cutlery. "Are we having lunch out here?"

"Yes, I thought we would." Angela released her daughter and ran an assessing glance over the dishes on the table. "Help me bring out the soup and the sandwiches, will you?"

"Sure, Mom." Melanie dropped her purse and keys onto a chair and followed her mother into the house.

"I hope you don't have to rush back to the Garden," Angela said over her shoulder as the two women returned to the deck moments later, each with their hands filled; Melanie carrying a soup tureen, and Angela handling a plate of sandwiches. "Just put that in the center of the table," Angela directed her, before they deposited their burdens and sat.

"No, Vickie is working this afternoon, so I can have a leisurely lunch." She smiled affectionately as her mother ladled out soup and poured iced tea. "I'm glad you called—we don't do this nearly often enough."

"And I'm glad you could come on such short notice. You're right, we shouldn't let ourselves get so busy with our lives that we don't have a chance to catch our breaths and visit.''

Melanie felt a twist of self-consciousness, aware that she hadn't had a chance to talk to her mother about Cole, and wondering what her father may have told her.

The table's striped umbrella cast its shade over the two as they ate lunch, chatting about a variety of things, until they finished eating and Angela had poured coffee into china cups.

When Angela leaned back in her chair and sipped her coffee while she eyed her daughter thoughtfully over the cup's gold-edged rim, Melanie knew the moment of truth had come. She braced herself, but when her mother didn't immediately say anything, she opened the subject they'd both been avoiding.

''I suppose Daddy told you that I've been seeing Cole McFadden?''

''Yes,'' her mother replied calmly, returning her cup to its saucer before her discerning blue glance moved back to Melanie's face. ''He told me that you'd decided to date him while he's visiting his parents.''

Melanie winced at her mother's choice of words.

''I don't want you and Daddy to worry about me, Mom. I know Cole is just visiting, and that when he's well enough to race, he'll be gone again. And I'll be left behind, just like before.''

''Is that what he told you? That he'll leave you and you won't hear from him again?''

''No.'' Melanie's gaze dropped to her cup and she moved it in slow circles in its saucer. ''No, that's not what he told me. He told me that he wants to give us a chance, that he wants a relationship."

"A relationship?" Angela's finely arched brows lifted in genuine confusion. "Just what in heavens name does that word *mean?* I hear it on television talk shows, I read it in articles in *Cosmopolitan*, but I still don't have a clear idea of its definition."

Melanie smiled wryly at her mother's baffled frown.

"I don't think it has a clear definition. As far as I can tell, it means different things to different people. And generally speaking, it's one of those words that means whatever you want it to mean."

Angela sniffed in well-bred disdain.

"In my day, people didn't have *relationships*. They either got married or they did not. Period." Her gaze narrowed shrewdly over her daughter's face. "What do you think the word means to Cole?"

"I'm not sure," Melanie gave her mother a small, helpless smile. "He says he doesn't want to have an affair."

"Hmmm," Angela said when Melanie's voice trailed off into silence and she seemed to forget her mother's presence as she stared distractedly at her fingers curled around the fragile cup. Her husband was worried sick about Melanie becoming involved with Cole again, and her own protective instincts were flashing warning signals. But unlike John, Angela had always suspected that much of Melanie's cool withdrawal from involvement with men was due to her love for Cole, which had never died—and perhaps, never would. So, she put aside her own instinctive urge to sweep her little girl away and guard her, and set about gently questioning Melanie. "And what about you, do you want to have an affair?"

"Mother!" Melanie's shocked gaze flew to meet her mother's tranquil, questioning stare. "How can you ask me something like that?"

"Very easily," Angela answered without batting an eyelash. "You're long past the stage where I have to treat you like a fourteen-year-old. And I like to think we're friends, as well as mother and daughter. Passion isn't something mothers are unacquainted with, my dear. How do you think you got here?"

"I always assumed I was left under a cabbage leaf," Melanie shot back, and was rewarded by a grin of pure deviltry from her mother. "Wasn't I?"

"No, Melanie, you were not," Angela said flatly, but her eyes danced with amusement. "Now that we have that out of the way, how do you feel about Cole?"

"I don't know," Melanie confessed.

"You've been seeing him regularly now for, how long?"

"Nightly for two weeks."

"Two weeks?" Angela lifted her eyebrows and thought back to her courting days with John. "Two weeks—and every night—that's a total of fourteen days," she mused, thinking out loud. "If I remember rightly, John would have been climbing the walls after two weeks."

"Mother!" Melanie flushed and stared at Angela, aghast.

"Melanie!" her mother chided softly, before she leaned forward, resting her forearms on the table. "What I'm trying to determine is whether you're saying no to something you desperately want for fear of being hurt. I've watched you hold men at arm's length since you were seventeen, Melanie. You're only interested in platonic relationships and you refuse to let a man into your life who expects anything more. I'm not saying I think you should become involved with Cole McFadden for purely physical reasons. But if he cares for you and you're afraid to give the two of you a chance because you're afraid of what *might* happen, then I have to tell you I hope you'll think long and hard about the real reason you're doing this. Is it because you don't want him or trust him? Or is it because you can't forget what happened when you were only seventeen and you're afraid of loving anyone ever again?"

"I don't know, Mom, I . . ." Melanie paused, staring at Angela. Was her mother right? She'd told her father she was an adult, not a fearful child, and that she was old enough to deal with her own life. She'd said basically the same thing to Cole, when she'd admitted she wanted him. But she was acting like a child, dithering over whether to say yes or no, refusing to decide. And the end result was she was wasting precious hours of the time she had left with Cole. Abruptly, she pushed back her chair and caught up her purse and keys before enveloping Angela in a quick, hard hug. "Thanks, Mom, you've been a big help."

"I have?" Angela felt as if she'd been caught up

in a tiny whirlwind. "What did I do?" she called after Melanie's departing back, as her daughter tossed her a wave and disappeared around the end of the house. Moments later, she heard the sound of Melanie's car reversing down the driveway. "Well, for heaven's sake," she murmured to herself, staring in consternation at the empty chair where Melanie had been only moments before. "What *did* I say?"

Melanie dialed the number with decisive movements, and paced back and forth in front of her desk while the phone rang.

"Hello?"

"Cole?"

"Yeah, this is Cole—Melanie?"

"Hi," she said, smiling with relief as his deep voice reached her ears.

"Hi," he answered, a bemused grin curving his mouth as he leaned against the wall by the refrigerator in his mom's kitchen. "I thought I wasn't going to get to talk to you until tonight."

"That's why I called, actually," Melanie said, suddenly nervous. "About tonight, I mean."

Cole's fingers tightened over the receiver, his muscles tensing.

"What about tonight? You're not cancelling, are you?"

"No, no—of course not!"

He sighed with relief and relaxed against the doorjamb.

"Good, because I'm counting the hours. So, what about tonight?"

Melanie nervously wound the telephone cord around her index finger.

"I thought I could," she faltered and drew a deep breath before starting again. "That is, I wondered if you'd like to have dinner at my house tonight, instead of going out to the Lakeshore?" There, she'd actually said it. She squeezed her eyes shut and held her breath. Would he understand? Or would she have to actually say the words.

Cole's heart stopped beating. Was she saying what he thought she was saying?

"I'd love to have dinner at your house," he said carefully, feeling his way through the mine field of emotions, littered with unspoken inferences, that pulsated over the wire. "Can I bring something? Wine, maybe?"

"That would be nice—maybe champagne?" her voice was unsteady, tentative.

"Champagne sounds great—I'll bring some," he said gravely, his voice reflecting none of the leaping elation that filled him.

"Good—then I'll see you at seven?"

"I'll be there with bells on. Bye, honey."

"Bye."

Melanie hung up the phone and pressed her palms against her midriff. Butterflies leapt and fluttered, trapped inside her stomach, and she felt nearly sick with nervous anticipation.

Cole hung up the phone. With a crow of exultation, he jumped upward and slapped the white-painted lintel over the door.

"Cole! For heaven's sake, what are you doing?"

Jeanie McFadden stopped midstride in the hallway and stared at her tall, broad-shouldered son.

"Celebrating, Mom, celebrating!" Cole reached her slim figure in three quick strides and caught her waist in his hands, swinging her off her feet and around in a circle before setting her down.

Jeanie shrieked in surprise, but before she could question him further he was gone, loping back down the hall, across the kitchen and the back porch on his way to buy champagne.

"These kids are going to drive me crazy," Jeanie muttered to herself as she wandered back into her office, righting her glasses on the bridge of her nose so she could return to reading the last four pages of a manuscript that had been due at her publisher three days before.

EIGHT

Cole tucked the bottle of champagne under his arm and shifted the bouquet of summer flowers before he rapped his knuckles against Melanie's screen door. The inner door that opened into the living room stood wide, the screen's mesh protection sheltering the rooms beyond from the mosquitoes that hovered and buzzed. The warm evening air was several degrees cooler than the humidity of afternoon, but Cole knew as June faded into July and July into August that the sun's heat would linger long after sunset.

The sound of footsteps against pine flooring echoed from inside the house and through the wire mesh of the screen. Cole watched Melanie enter the living room and walk toward him. The full skirt of the scoop-necked sundress she wore swayed rhythmically as she walked, the soft rose cotton echoing the flush of color in her cheeks as she pushed open the screen door.

"Hi," she said, her voice sounding throaty and vaguely breathless. "You're right on time."

"Hi." Cole stepped across the threshold, letting the door slap shut behind him before he bent and brushed a kiss against her cheek and the corner of her mouth.

Melanie closed her eyes and leaned into the warm strength of his body. Her arms slid around his waist and she pressed against him, some of her fears calmed by the strong, solid feel of him. She buried her face against the tanned column of his throat, inhaling the clean smell of soap and aftershave.

"Uhmmm," she said, sighing as she breathed in the familiar aromas added to the scent of male that was uniquely Cole. "You smell wonderful."

Cole laughed, hugging her against him with his hands still full of the champagne bottle and flowers. He dropped his face against the silky fall of loosened hair at her temple, drawing in the scent of perfume, powder, and shampoo.

"That's supposed to be my line," he chuckled, "and it's true—you smell wonderful."

Melanie smiled, her lips moving against the warm skin of his throat. They stood motionless for long moments, luxuriating in the fit of body against body. And for the first time since her telephone call, she relaxed. Unfortunately, all too soon her frazzled nerves made their presence known, and she stepped back and out of his arms.

"Are those for me?" she asked, avoiding his eyes

as she gestured at the colorful bouquet wrapped in green florist's paper.

"Yes," he answered and held out the flowers. While she lowered her nose to the fragrant blooms, he lifted the bottle in his other hand. "And this is for both of us."

Melanie read the label and gasped, her wide green eyes lifting quickly to his.

"Dom Perignon! My goodness, Cole, it's so expensive! You shouldn't have!"

"Why not?" he asked lazily. His deep voice held shades of meaning echoed in the blue eyes that searched hers. "Don't we have something to celebrate tonight?"

Melanie couldn't bring herself to answer him, but neither could she lie.

"I'm just not sure if Dom Perignon goes with steak and baked potatoes."

Cole allowed her the small evasion and followed her as she led the way into the kitchen. He leaned against the doorjamb and watched as she bent to remove a vase from a lower cabinet and ran cold water from the tap to fill it.

"I checked the potatoes a few minutes ago, and they're not quite done." She knew she was chattering, but she couldn't seem to stop herself. "I hope you're not starving because it may be another twenty minutes before we can eat."

"No problem," Cole answered, watching her arrange the flowers in the vase, his eyes narrowing over the trembling in her fingers. "Why don't I open the champagne while we're waiting."

"Yes—that's a wonderful idea," Melanie said brightly, and groaned inwardly. She was acting like a fifteen-year-old on her first date, but she couldn't seem to stop the fluttering in her midsection that threatened to set her whole body quaking. Cole unpeeled the gold foil protecting the bottle's corked top and she quickly left the kitchen for the little dining area just off the living room. She painstakingly centered the vase of flowers in the precise center of the table and double-checked the two place settings of china, crystal, and silverware. Everything was in its proper place, just as it had been the last five times she'd checked it before Cole's arrival. *Calm down,* she ordered the butterflies in her stomach, and pressed a shaky hand against the rose cotton covering her navel. *We'll eat dinner and then when we're both more relaxed, things will progress naturally. I hope.* She drew a deep breath, squared her shoulders, and walked back into the kitchen.

Cole was pouring the champagne into two stemmed crystal glasses, and looked up as she entered.

"Perfect timing," he commented, and held out one of the glasses. She took it and he lifted his glass, his gaze holding hers with compelling warmth. "To us."

"To us," Melanie echoed, and sipped. The wine was smooth, with a faint bite. It occurred to her that it might soothe the ragged edges of her nerves, so she tipped the glass up again and drained it. "May I have some more?"

"Uh, sure." Cole refilled her glass, watched her

quickly down her second glass of champagne as if it were a badly needed dose of medicine, and realized his plan for a slow seduction, following a leisurely dinner with wine, might not be workable. Melanie was so nervous that when he'd held her, he'd felt the fine tremor that shook her slim frame. He wasn't at all sure she would make it through dinner without bursting into tears. He eyed her thoughtfully as she set her empty glass down atop the cabinet and grabbed a potholder.

"I thought we could barbecue the steaks on the grill outside," she said in a rush of words, as she pulled open the oven door and peered inside to test one of the potatoes with a fork. "I lit the briquettes some time ago, but if you want to check them for me—maybe we should start the steaks."

Cole heard the forced brightness in her voice and made up his mind. She wouldn't make it through dinner and he couldn't stand watching her work herself into a nervous breakdown agonizing over something that should be as natural as life itself.

"Melanie," he said softly.

She stiffened at the sound of his voice and stood upright, closing the oven door before turning slowly to face him. His face held understanding and a banked heat that simmered in the depths of his eyes. Something strung tightly inside her began to slowly unwind.

His gaze held hers as he silently reached out and took the potholder from her slack fingers to drop it back on top of the cabinet, gently crowding her when he stepped closer to reach around her and turn off the oven. His hands settled on either side of her waist and he moved her to the left until she felt the wall at her back. Her hands came to rest on the waistband of his jeans.

"What . . ." she whispered, stopping to wet her lips and try again. "What are you doing?"

Cole smiled, a small upward tilting of his lips.

Melanie's gaze flicked from his eyes to his mouth, before returning with helpless fascination to his eyes again. He shifted closer, planting both palms flat against the wall on each side of her head while he slowly aligned his lower body against hers. Melanie's heart began a slow steady thud of anticipation at the feel of his warm weight settling against her and the leap of blue fire in the eyes fastened on hers.

"Cole . . ." she breathed, her fingers tightening in unbearable tension against the muscles of his waist.

"If you don't want this," he said, his voice strained with the effort it took to hold his body in check, "now's the time to say no."

"No," she answered quickly.

He went completely still, disbelief and disappointment flaring in his eyes.

"No?" he repeated softly, his body rigid with denial.

"Not *no*, I don't want this," Melanie hastened to explain. "I mean, *no*, I don't want to say no."

"Does that mean yes, you want me? Now?" Cole was having trouble thinking when his body was shrieking for attention.

"Yes." Melanie reached up and smoothed away

the frown of confusion that drew lines between his brows.

"Thank God." He breathed with relief before he dropped his head the scant inches that separated them and took her mouth with his.

Melanie slid her arms around his neck and tugged him closer, welcoming with feverish pleasure the heavy weight of his body that pinned her against the wall. Nerves that had earlier been frazzled now hummed with excitement and anticipation. His mouth slanted against hers and for long moments the slow swaying movements of body pressed to body, and the heated pressure of mouth against mouth was enough. But then his tongue nudged the seam of her lips, her mouth opened beneath his, and his tongue pushed into the warm, wet hollow beyond.

The fast pound of his heartbeat drummed in Cole's ears, deafening him, and he fought to hold onto his fast-slipping control. The soft welcoming curve of Melanie's body giving way beneath his and the warm slide of her arms around his neck was bearable, but the hot, honeyed warmth of her mouth was his undoing. She sucked eagerly on his tongue and the soft little moans coming from the back of her throat echoed the frantic twisting of her body against his.

Without lifting his mouth from hers, Cole slid an arm around her shoulders and bent to find the back of her thighs with his other hand to swing her off her feet and into his arms. Melanie barely gasped at the sudden move, so absorbed was she with the fire that sang through her veins and fogged her mind to anything outside the reality of Cole's arms.

Cole reluctantly lifted his mouth from hers. She buried her face against his neck, her tongue drawing tasting circles against his skin as his long strides carried them down the hallway and into her bedroom. He released her and her body slid with tantalizing slowness down his, stoking the fires that raged through every muscle of his body. He lowered his mouth to claim a quick, fierce kiss before he lifted his lips and tilted his head back so he could search her face. His fingers fanned over her throat, his thumb compulsively smoothing her bottom lip.

"I wanted to give you champagne, moonlight, and roses," his voice was gravelly, taut with the iron control he struggled to maintain.

Melanie read the concern for her that fought with the naked need that lay deep in his blue eyes and tightened the skin over the hard bone structure of his face.

"I already had champagne," she whispered softly, "and I don't need moonlight and roses. All I need is you." Knowing that the same exquisite pain of desire that tortured her was attacking him, gave her confidence, and her lips curved in a smile beneath his stroking thumb. Her hands slid from his neck and with slow, purposeful movements, she tugged the hem of his shirt from his jeans and pulled the white knit upwards.

She'd planned to pull it completely off, but each inch upward exposed more of his tanned, warm, muscled body, and she deserted his shirt to lean forward and bury her lips against his chest.

Cole drew air into lungs suddenly needing oxygen

when she let go of his shirt and wrapped her arms around his bare torso. The washboard muscles across his midriff clenched and he gasped out loud when her hair shifted across his skin and her tongue flicked out to move in exploring, tasting swirls until it found the flat, brown disk of his nipple.

"Melanie," he groaned and caught the edge of his shirt to rip it off over his head. He tossed it behind him and wrapped his arms around her, his fingers tangling in the thick black silk of her hair to press her tighter against him. His other hand moved restlessly over her back, but was frustrated by the cotton covering that kept him from the satiny smoothness of her skin.

"How do I get you out of this," he said, his voice rasping huskily against her ear.

"Mmmmh," Melanie murmured, absorbed in her exploration of the satiny muscles bared to the touch of her mouth and fingers. "Side zipper—under my arm."

Cole's fingers moved unerringly to the hidden placket, but were sidetracked by the swell of her breast as he slid the zipper downward, loosening the top of her dress. He groaned and grabbed the rose skirt, bunching it in his hands as he frantically pulled it upward.

"Lift your arms," he instructed, and Melanie complied. But her legs refused to hold her upright and Cole had to support her while he pulled the dress up her body and off over her head, tugging it from between the press of their bodies. The dress, too, was tossed over his shoulder and forgotten. He nearly stopped breathing when he looked down at Melanie. Supported by his hand at her waist, she swayed on her feet, clad only in a brief lacy bra and a matching tiny scrap of cream lace and satin, which covered the smoky black curls that were just barely visible between her legs.

She straightened and her fingers clutched at his arm as she stepped out of the strappy pink sandals that covered her feet.

Slowly, Cole kicked off his loafers and his hand moved to unsnap his jeans, the slide of the zipper a loud rasp in the heated silence of the bedroom.

Melanie moaned, a soft sound that caught in the back of her throat, overwhelmed by the tide of hot desire that swept her. She leaned her forehead against him, the flat of her palm lying against the heated skin of his midriff. She felt the ripple of reaction that clenched his muscles beneath her hand, before her fingers slid into the v'd opening of his jeans and found him.

Every nerve in Cole's body screamed with elation, every muscle in his body jerked with reaction.

"Yes," he ground out, his eyes closing, his jaw clenching with unbearable pleasure. "Touch me, Melanie, touch me."

He stood it for as long as he could, unwilling to end the incredible pleasure of her soft hand moving with shy, searching strokes against him. But it had been too long and he wanted her too badly. He picked her up and laid her on the bed, quickly stripping off his jeans, shorts, and socks before following her down to blanket her body with his.

"Next time," he promised, his voice slurred and guttural, "next time we'll go slow." And his lips covered hers, his tongue surging into her mouth in a rhythm echoed by the slow movements of his hips against hers. He reached down and caught the lace of her panties and stripped them down her legs with one swift stroke while she clung to him, her shoulders lifting off the bed to keep his mouth from deserting hers. "It's okay, baby, I'm not going anywhere," he assured her, his fingers pausing to tangle in the triangle of black silk between her legs. Melanie gasped in pleasure and his eyes, already heavy-lidded, flared with heat. He leaned away from her to find his jeans on the floor, took out a packet, and ripped the cover off with his teeth. Seconds later, he settled heavily between her thighs and with one swift surge, joined them.

It was heaven. It was hell. He didn't want to move for fear it would end too soon. But if he didn't move, he'd surely die. He gritted his teeth and leaned his forehead against hers.

On some level, Melanie knew he teetered on the edge, but she couldn't control the tiny contractions of inner muscles that caressed the hard length of him joined to her. She moaned, her hips lifting in an unconscious plea.

"Don't move," Cole managed to get out. "Honey, don't move or this will all be over." *And I want to stay inside you forever*, he realized with agonizing clarity.

But it was too late. Her fingers clutched at his shoulders, her mouth was wild as it moved across his cheek in search of his. And Cole gave in, wrapping her tightly against him and letting the hot tide of desire swamp him as she lured him under, both of them out of control as each fed the other's need.

Long explosive moments later, Cole lifted his head from the warm curve of her throat and levered his weight up and away from the fragile woman he held. She murmured in protest, her arms clinging, fingers tightening against the sweat-dampened skin of his back.

"Don't go," she whispered. Her face was soft with sated passion, her eyes closed, the thick brush of her lashes making dark crescents against the delicate skin under her eyes.

"I'm not going anywhere," Cole murmured reassuringly, his fingers brushing a lock of black hair from her cheek and smoothing it against the stark white of the pillowcase. His fingertips traced the planes and curves of her face with gentle tenderness. And when they smoothed with a butterfly touch over her eyelids and brushed the tips of her eyelashes, Melanie opened her eyes and looked up at him.

The depth of emotion that lay in his blue gaze was underlaid with a hint of awed wonder that echoed the storm of feelings in her own heart. Tears slowly welled and overflowed, tracing liquid trails from the corners of her eyes.

"Honey? What's wrong?" Panic hit Cole and he swiftly cursed his lack of control. Even as crazy with desire as he'd been, he'd known the moment his body entered hers that it had been a long time since she'd made love. "Did I hurt you? What is it? Damn it, I did hurt you, didn't I?"

"No." Melanie smiled hazily up at his worried face, hugging him tighter, loving the crush of his lower torso against hers, the muscled length of his legs aligned with hers. "It's just that it's been so long since I've held you like this, and," her voice faltered and Cole bent closer to hear her, "I've missed you so much."

Her words slammed into Cole's heart, and there was a suspicious dampness in his own eyes when he answered her, his lips brushing hers as he spoke. "I've missed you, too, sweetheart—every day, every hour, every minute since the last time we were together like this."

His lashes drifted lower and his lips covered hers, moving against the soft, swollen outline of her mouth with a tender reverence that brought fresh tears to dampen her soft skin.

"Don't cry, baby, don't cry," he whispered against her mouth, his lips moving to lick the salty dampness from her skin. "I want you to be happy, not sad."

"I am happy," she managed to get out, closing her eyes with a groan of pleasure at the faintly raspy strokes of his tongue against her skin. He shifted against her and she gasped, the movement stealing her breath. Her hips lifted in subtle response and his body reacted with growing arousal. "Cole," she whispered, her voice holding a sultry heat that sent his blood shuddering through his veins, "make love to me again."

Cole didn't bother to answer her. His body's response was all the answer she needed, and together they fell back into the deep well of hot pleasure that lured them.

It was three a.m. Cole could read the luminous numbers on the clock radio on the table beside the bed. He lay awake, staring at the ceiling of Melanie's bedroom. Exhausted, she lay sleeping in his arms, the curves of her body bare and warm against his own naked skin as she snuggled against him, her head on his shoulder, one hand curled against his chest, her leg flung across his with her knee drawn up to nudge his thigh.

He'd lost count of the number of times they'd made love. Melanie had finally fallen asleep, but Cole was wide awake. Even if he'd been drowsy, he would have fought sleep because he couldn't bear to waste even one minute of this night with her. She was summer heat and liquid lightning, wise woman and vulnerable girl, and she had the same ability to make all the pieces of his world fall into place that she'd had eight years before.

Cole turned his face to press his lips against the crown of her head and its covering of silky black hair that rested just below his chin. His arms tightened around her slim form and she murmured in her sleep, her own arms unconsciously returning his hug. With the blinding clarity that sometimes reaches people in the pre-dawn hours, Cole admitted to himself that he had never stopped loving her. And after the last few weeks, his love for Melanie, the girl she'd been, had melded with a new love for Melanie, the woman she'd become. He tilted his head back so he could see her face, his fingertips tracing her delicate, beloved features while he slowly became accustomed to the wonder and peace that filled his heart.

Melanie woke to the brush of Cole's fingers stroking her face. She smiled contentedly, her eyes opening slowly to find him watching her while his hand cupped her cheek.

"Hello," she whispered, reaching up to trace his lower lip with a lazy forefinger. "Can't you sleep?"

"No." He shook his head, a small movement against the pillow that further tousled the tawny thickness of his hair. "I don't want to."

"Why not? Aren't you tired? What have you been doing while I've been asleep?" Loving fingers smoothed back a lock of sun-streaked blonde hair that fell over his brow, before stroking back down his cheek. Her fingernail rasped against the early morning stubble covering his cheek and jaw, and she smiled.

"I've been lying here watching you sleep—and thinking how much I love you."

The words stilled Melanie's fingers against his face and wiped the sleepy smile from her lips. Her eyes widened and her gaze searched his face. But the intent blue eyes fastened on hers held no hint of teasing.

"Cole—I don't know what to say . . ." she said helplessly.

"You don't have to say anything—unless you want to tell me that you feel the same way," he said, his voice a husky rasp in the quiet room.

"I'm not sure what I feel," she said slowly, her voice hesitant. Somewhere deep inside her, a tiny bud of hope, long frozen and repressed, began to slowly unfurl. Did she dare believe him? "I know that I enjoy being with you and when we make love—it feels so right. But . . . do I have to know right this moment? Can't we just enjoy being together without the pressure of promises of love?"

"Is it because you don't believe me?" he asked, disappointed at her reply but not really surprised.

"Maybe—I'm just not ready for promises of tomorrow, Cole."

Cole read the worry in the green eyes lifted to his. With a sensitivity to her wariness that would have surprised her had she known, he accepted the fact that only time would convince her that his loving her would have a different ending this time around.

"Okay," he said. "You don't have to promise me forever. But I'm going to tell you that I love you every chance I get until you realize that this time is different. We have a second chance, and this time I'm not letting you get away."

Melanie still wasn't convinced, but any protest she would have uttered was forgotten when Cole wrapped his arms around her, rolled her onto her back, and kissed her.

Cole kissed Melanie good-bye and reluctantly let her leave to open Victoria's Garden at a quarter to ten the next morning. It was already warm and growing warmer outside her house as Cole padded barefooted back upstairs to take his shower and get dressed.

He felt a faint twinge of guilt that he hadn't told Melanie what he planned to do. He didn't know if she would have objected, but he knew without a doubt that whether she did or didn't, this was something he had to do. This time around, his courting of Melanie was going to be proper and aboveboard.

And to that end, he was going to pay a visit to John Winters and ask him for his daughter's hand in marriage, and hopefully mend the bridges that had been burnt all those years ago. He couldn't have his future father-in-law running him off his property with a shotgun.

Angela answered the knock at the Winters' lakeside home, and her eyes widened in shock when she recognized the broad-shouldered man standing on her porch, the screen door separating them.

"Yes?" she managed to get out.

"Good morning, Mrs. Winters," Cole said gravely. "Is your husband at home?"

"Yes, he is," she responded dazedly, nonplussed, "but I'm not sure . . ."

"I'd like to speak to him, if I may," Cole said with quiet firmness.

Angela stared at Cole for a long moment. Except for photographs and interviews on television, this was the first opportunity she'd had to see the man her daughter loved. Her shrewd blue gaze flicked over the conservative tan slacks and white linen shirt unbuttoned at the throat, the polished brown loafers, and the gold Rolex on his wrist. She looked beyond the handsome features to the integrity and mature strength that lay in the depths of his eyes and the determined set of his chin, and made up her mind.

"Very well," she said with calm decision. "Come in."

"Thank you." Cole knew she was gauging him. And although he didn't know what swung the pendulum in his favor, he knew she'd decided to accept him when the blue eyes warmed and the faintly hostile stiffness of her slim figure relaxed. He stepped over the threshold and followed her across the hall to an old-fashioned parlor where John Winters sat in an overstuffed armchair near a fireplace, its cold grate filled with summer flowers.

"John," Angela's voice drew her husband's attention. Distracted from his absorption in a leatherbound book, his eyes left the thick volume, his head turning toward her. "There's someone here to see you."

The emerald eyes so like Melanie's swept with mild curiosity to glance beyond her, but when he recognized Cole, they blazed with instant anger.

"Why did you let him in here?" he demanded abruptly, his gaze flashing with accusing swiftness to his wife.

"Because he wanted to see you," she said with unshakable composure, "and I think you should see him."

"Hah!" John Winters snorted, pushing upright from his chair.

"John—" Angela said warningly, an admonishing look reminding him of his reluctant agreement to let

Melanie handle her involvement with Cole in her own way.

"All right, all right," her husband answered testily. He turned to toss the book against the soft cushions of the chair before swinging back to face Cole, his hands propped belligerently on his hips. "What do you want?" he demanded.

Cole was no longer a heartbroken youngster. He was eight years older, eight years harder, and he'd long since learned to swim with the sharks. He wasn't intimidated by the older man's anger, and the blue eyes that met John's hot green were calm and cool.

"I want to marry your daughter," he said with quiet politeness, "and I'd like to ask for your blessing."

"What?" John stared at him, red color surging up his throat to suffuse his face. "Well, you're a dollar short and about eight years too late!"

"I'm sorry about what happened eight years ago," Cole said with commendable calm in the face of the older man's ire, "but I loved her then and I love her now. I would have married her if she'd been older, but I didn't think it was fair of me to ask her to give up her youth and settle down when she was so young. I didn't want to ruin her plans for college and . . ."

"Ruin her plans?" Winters interrupted with an expletive. "I suppose you don't think being pregnant ruined her plans?"

"Pregnant?" Cole felt as if he'd been slugged in

the solar plexus. His brain froze and refused to function. "What do you mean—pregnant?"

"I mean pregnant—as in she was going to have a baby. Your baby."

"My God," Cole whispered, the blood draining from his face as he stared at Melanie's father.

"John," Angela interjected, reading the shock and disbelief on Cole's pale face.

"And then we almost lost her. She damn near bled to death that Christmas—and where the hell were you? I'll tell you where you weren't, you weren't here! You got her pregnant and then you dumped her—you didn't even have the guts to call her. You sent her a letter! Left her alone and pregnant with your baby—and she was barely more than a baby herself!"

"John," Angela's hand closed over his arm and she shook him gently but insistently.

"What?" he snarled, turning to look impatiently down into her worried face.

"He didn't know."

"Of course, he knew! He . . ." John's angry eyes moved back to Cole's blank eyes and white face, and he swiftly reassessed his claim. "You did know, didn't you?"

"What happened?" Cole asked, his voice raw with the pain that clawed at his chest. The blue gaze fastened on the older couple was tormented.

"She miscarried," Angela said gently, and with a pleading look at her husband, she stepped next to Cole and caught his arm. "Sit down, Cole. I can see that this has been a shock. John," she glanced at her husband as she steered a stunned Cole to an armchair, "I think a drink of brandy would help."

"Yeah, all right." For eight years, John Winters had dreamed of revenge and the opportunity to confront the man who had so callously destroyed his daughter's innocence, but now that he had, his anger was gone and he could only feel pity for the grief-stricken younger man.

Glass clinked against glass, liquid gurgled, and then someone pushed a tumbler half full of amber liquid into Cole's hand. He sat staring at it, unable to remember what it was for or how it got there.

"Drink it, son, it'll help."

Cole obeyed the gruff voice and tipped the glass. The liquor burnt as it went down, warming insides that had gone cold as ice. He cleared his throat twice before he could make his vocal chords work.

"Was she—is she . . ." his voice rasped to a halt, sudden tears clogging his throat and halting his speech. Cool, slender fingers covered his where his hand clenched into a fist against his thigh and he glanced up to find Melanie's mother perched on the arm of his chair. The blue eyes that met his were filled with sympathetic understanding.

"Melanie was very ill for a period of time, but she healed perfectly. She wasn't left with any aftereffects—she can have more children, if she wishes." Angela's voice gentled further. "The baby was a boy—she grieved for his loss."

"Oh, God," Cole's throat closed over the words and he squeezed his eyes shut. "A boy. And I left her alone." His voice echoed the agony that contorted his features and when his lashes lifted, the gaze that met Angela's held all the torments of hell. "I have to go." He lurched upright and fumbled the glass onto a small walnut table.

"Are you sure you should be driving?" Angela asked worriedly, John a few steps behind her as she followed Cole to the door.

"Yeah, I'm fine," he managed to reply. He pushed open the door and stepped out onto the porch.

Angela and John watched him cross the lawn and heaved a sigh of relief when he negotiated the drive with easy control.

"Thank God that man's a professional driver," John muttered, his gaze following the vintage Thunderbird as it turned onto the highway. "I'd hate like hell to have to drive in his condition."

Angela's blue eyes searched her husband's face.

"I think maybe we've been wrong about that young man," she said and was rewarded with a slow nod of agreement from John.

"I think you may be right," he said reluctantly.

"I also think I better call Melanie—she's working this morning, but in my opinion that young man of hers needs her."

John held the screen door for his wife and followed her back into the house, his brow creasing in a thoughtful frown.

NINE

Cole didn't remember the drive from the lake to Melanie's house in town. He didn't even question why Melanie's car was sitting in the drive when she'd left for work only two hours before. He pulled the Thunderbird in behind her little Toyota and twisted the ignition key to kill the engine. For a long moment, he sat motionless, staring unseeingly at the back of the car parked in front of him, before he slid out and made his way with slow steps up the walkway and across the porch. Blind instinct had led him this far, but as he stared at her front door, he suddenly realized he had no idea what he was going to say to her. What could he say? He'd once unthinkingly destroyed her life, and then returned to shove his way back into her world and demand that she love him again.

God, what an arrogant bastard I am, he thought with a twist of self-disgust. *I'm lucky she even speaks to me.*

Melanie watched his car pull into her drive, her nerves tightening with apprehension when he didn't immediately get out. Was he angry? She couldn't see his expression as he walked slowly toward the house. If he was furious with her for not telling him about the baby, she couldn't blame him. She'd meant to tell him last night, but somehow each time she searched for the words, she'd been sidetracked by their lovemaking. Her mother had said he was very upset. But Melanie had been in such a hurry to leave the shop and go home, she hadn't taken the time to quiz Angela as to just exactly what she meant by *upset*.

His footsteps paused on the porch, but there was no rap of knuckles against the door. Melanie didn't wait for him to knock. She pulled the door open to find him standing on the other side and all thoughts of his anger fled as she saw the pain that ravaged his beloved features.

"Cole," she breathed, her heart aching with compassion for the grief and loss she read in his eyes. She pushed open the screen door and held it wide, reaching out a hand to catch his and pull him inside.

The frozen ice that gripped him warmed slightly under her touch. His gaze probed hers, and he was only dimly aware that she'd pushed the door shut behind them, closing them away inside the privacy of the house walls. The green eyes held a reflection of his own pain, but not hate. Still, he couldn't believe she didn't harbor resentment toward him.

"I'm so sorry, honey," his voice was raspy with unshed tears. "I'm so damn sorry."

Melanie stepped into his arms, wrapping him close and holding him tight in an effort to keep the dragon talons of regret and remorse at bay.

Cole squeezed his eyes shut in an effort to hold back the tears that hovered behind his lashes. He hadn't cried since he was ten and his best friend for nine years, a collie named Casey, had died. His arms closed around Melanie's slim form with punishing force, absorbing her heat in an attempt to melt the cold that overwhelmed him.

Melanie barely noticed the painful crush of his grip. She held him tighter in a vain attempt to relieve the grief and heartbreak she recognized so easily. She'd had eight years to grow accustomed to the loss of their child, but for Cole, the shock and grief were brand new.

"You must hate me," he said, his words muffled as his lips moved against her hair.

"No," she said, her voice underlaid with gentle surety. "I don't hate you. Not now."

"Did you then—when you lost the baby?"

"Yes."

Cole winced, the single word a blow that his body flinched away from.

"But I hated the whole world then—I was even angry at God for taking him away. I was scared to death when I found out I was pregnant, but I wanted the baby so badly. I don't think I realized how desperately I wanted him until I woke up in the hospital and they told me I'd miscarried and there wouldn't be a baby after all."

Cole drew a deep, shuddering breath, his chest falling and rising slowly beneath Melanie's cheek. She tilted her face back to look up at him, her hair shifting in a silky fall over the tight circle of his arms.

"You're not angry that I didn't tell you?"

"Angry? No, I'm not angry—I don't have the right to be angry. If I'd been more careful, you wouldn't have been in that situation."

"It takes two people to make a baby, Cole," she said gently. As she said the words, Melanie realized that, after all the years of harboring hurt and bitterness, she truly meant them. A surge of relief hit her as she felt her heart lift in a swift rush of freedom.

"True, but I was older than you—I should have made sure that you were protected." With a familiar ease that seemed right, he slipped an arm under her thighs and swung her up into his arms. When she looked at him questioningly, he answered her unvoiced query with a voice that rasped with emotion. "I want to lie down and hold you—if that's all right with you?"

Melanie knew that if she said no, he wouldn't insist. She knew he was really asking if their long night of lovemaking and the earthshaking revelations of the morning had moved their relationship to a deeper level, one in which he was allowed to take for granted her willingness to grant him the privileges of a lover.

"Yes—that's all right with me."

Cole didn't say anything, but the lock of his blue eyes on hers spoke volumes. When he laid her on the bed and came down beside her to gather her against the long length of him, she closed her eyes against the sweet surge of emotion that swept her.

"When I found out I was pregnant, the first thought I had was that I wanted you there to hold me," she said unsteadily, her face snuggled against the warm curve of his throat, "just like this."

"I would have been there to hold you," he said rustily, his arms tightening. "Knowing that you needed me and I wasn't there tears me apart. I would never have let you go through that alone."

"I know," she whispered, wrapping him closer.

He leaned up on an elbow and looked down at her to search her face, before his gaze moved down her body. His hand lifted, his palm smoothing with gentle reverence over the flat plane of her abdomen.

"We'll have other babies, Melanie," he vowed softly. The blue eyes that swept back up to meet hers held a tender promise. "A little boy to replace the one we lost. And I'll take such good care of you and the baby, I promise."

Melanie couldn't stop the tears that welled to spill over and track damp trails down her cheeks.

"Don't cry." Pain flickered in his eyes and his thumb caught the salty drops. "I've caused you enough pain, I don't ever want to hurt you again. I love you."

His lips brushed hers once, twice, before his mouth settled over hers. Melanie gave up trying to unsnarl her tangled emotions and surrendered to his tender seduction. Part of her leapt with hope that this time the love he offered her would last forever, but her still-cautious heart warned her to be careful.

Melanie woke the next morning and for a moment frowned in confusion at the muscled chest her cheek rested against, before she remembered Cole had spent the night. She murmured a satisfied sigh and snuggled against him.

"Hey," he said softly, tightening his arms around her. "Are you awake?"

"No," she denied abruptly, her voice husky with early-morning roughness.

Cole smiled, one hand smoothing over the soft warm curves pressed tightly against his own hard frame.

"Does that mean I couldn't interest you in coffee and maple bars?" he asked, his voice a gentle rumble beneath her ear. There was a barely perceptible tensing of the body lying against his as she considered his offer.

"No," she mumbled, burrowing closer.

"If you'll wake up and go to church with me this morning, I'll buy you coffee and maple bars," he said, trying to bribe her without feeling a qualm of remorse.

She lay silently for a moment, considering his offer.

"Promise?"

"I promise."

"Oh, all right," she grumbled and reluctantly unwound her body from his and tossed back the covers.

Cole clasped his hands behind his head and unashamedly watched as she rose from the bed, naked as the day she was born, and stumbled to the bathroom. He grinned with appreciation at the tempting sight. One nice thing about having a woman who didn't wake up fast, he mused, was that she was too asleep to realize he was ogling her.

She disappeared through the bathroom door and he pushed out of bed to follow her.

Maybe she needs help washing her back, he thought with a wicked grin, and disappeared through the bathroom door after her.

Melanie was standing with her face turned up to the shower spray, eyes closed as the water sluiced over her, when Cole stepped silently into the shower stall behind her.

Warm, wet hands slid around her waist and she yelped in shock, her eyes flying open only to be filled with water.

Cole laughed and steadied her when she staggered.

"What are you doing?" she managed to get out as she wiped the water out of her eyes and shot him a fulminating glare over her shoulder.

"I'm going to wash your back for you," he said with an innocent smile. "I thought it would be a good way to prove to you how helpful I can be around the house."

"Vacuuming my rugs and washing the windows is being *helpful around the house*," she said with an accusing frown that told him she wasn't buying any of it. "Sharing my shower doesn't fall under that category."

He eyed her with interest. Her black hair was slicked back from her face, her delicate features bare of makeup and still every bit as beautiful.

"Really? What category does it fall under?"

Seduction. The word popped immediately into her mind, and she stared at him without speaking.

"What?" he lifted an eyebrow.

"Nothing," she turned her back on him and picked up the soap.

"No, that was a *something* look, not nothing." One wet palm closed over her shoulder and he turned her back to face him. "Come on, tell me."

The look she gave him from beneath the sweep of long black lashes was sultry and inviting, and it stole his breath.

"Seduction," she said, leaning toward him until the tips of her breasts grazed his chest. One soap-covered hand slid down his chest and across the muscles of his midriff with agonizing slowness, until her fingers reached their destination below his waist. "Climbing into my shower wearing nothing but your birthday suit definitely falls into the category of seduction, Mr. McFadden," she whispered. "Is that what you had in mind?"

"Yeah," he managed to get out. "Something like that."

"Oh, good." She smiled, all foggy sleepiness gone from her expressive features. "I was hoping you'd say that."

A half hour later, Cole stepped into the bedroom,

a bath towel wrapped around his waist, another in his hands as he towel dried his hair and eyed Melanie's slim figure in a pale pink bra and matching half-slip. She was seated in front of an old-fashioned dressing table, brushing her long mane of hair until it fell sleekly over her shoulders and down her back.

"You know," he said suspiciously, "sometimes I'm not sure who's seducing who here."

"Whom," she responded with a final flick of the brush through her hair. "Who's seducing whom."

"Yeah, well, whatever," he said with a frown. "Don't interrupt. Just whose idea was it to seduce whom in that shower?"

Melanie smiled at his reflection in the mirror and stood, shaking her hair loose down her back as she stepped away from the brocade-covered stool and walked to the closet.

"I think maybe it was mutual, don't you?"

"Maybe," Cole agreed, not completely convinced. For a moment, he considered that maybe, just maybe, she'd known he was watching her when she walked naked into the bathroom.

Melanie smiled, a soft little upward curve of her mouth, into the depths of her closet. It was never a good idea to let a man think he knew exactly what was going on, she reflected with satisfaction. A little mystery never hurt. She wasn't planning to confess that she'd staggered half-asleep into the bathroom, but the sight of him wet and half-aroused in the confines of the shower, the steam from the water misting the air between them, had shocked her from sleepiness to desire in one short breath.

Greater Coventry ARC
Physician Orders

NAME: Laura Galo **Allergic to: (indicate in red)**	"Renew" m signature c and those v signature i page have Group Hon for 90 days

Sunday

dishes
vacuum
sign cards
put books back

Cole was still not sure who seduced whom when he stood aside to let Melanie precede him into his family's pew at Grace Lutheran Church a short hour later.

Gavin McFadden, Cole's father, leaned sideways to whisper in his wife's ear.

"Is she the one who rated champagne?"

Jeanie smiled, grey eyes sparkling as she reached up to whisper back.

"I don't know, but I hope so. Wouldn't it be lovely if they got married?"

Gavin's inelegant snort earned him a swift pinch in the ribs.

"Stop pinching me!" he whispered. "You've got marriage on the brain. Just because he brought her to church with him doesn't mean he plans to marry her!"

Jeanie leaned unobtrusively forward to glance down the pew at her oldest son. She was rewarded by a glimpse of tender, unadulterated adoration on his face as he handed Melanie a hymnal and smiled down at her. Jeanie settled comfortably back against the wooden pew and slipped a hand through the crook of her husband's arm. Once again, she reached up to whisper in his ear.

"Wanna bet?"

The entire McFadden clan gathered at Gavin and Jeanie's house after church. Jeanie was in the kitchen, taking cold cuts and potato salad out of the refrigerator when Cole and Melanie walked in the back door.

"Hi, Mom, what's for lunch?" Cole asked, reaching a long arm over her shoulder and snitching a slice of honey-cured ham from the platter in her hand.

"Cold cuts, fried chicken, watermelon—the usual picnic fare." She slid the platter onto the work table in the center of the old-fashioned kitchen and slapped his fingers away when he reached for a second slice. "Stop that—you'll have to wait till I get it on the table, just like everyone else." She smiled at the slim brunette standing just inside the back door. "Hello, again, Melanie. I'm so glad you two decided to join us for lunch."

"Yeah—we haven't seen Cole a lot during the last few weeks," Gavin's voice boomed and Melanie looked past Jeanie to see Cole's father's broad-shouldered figure standing in the doorway. It was easy to see where the younger McFaddens got their blonde hair and lake-blue eyes. Just now, Gavin's blue eyes were twinkling with teasing mischief. "I can see why—if I were twenty years younger—"

"Hah," Jeanie scoffed without heat. "Maybe twenty-five or thirty!"

"I don't know, Mom," Cole said, the grin quirking his lips in a replica of his father's cocky smile. "You should see the women hanging around him down at the shop. I think they loosen bolts in their car engines on purpose, just for an excuse to talk to him."

Jeanie's thick brown lashes narrowed over grey eyes and she frowned threateningly at the two men. "Is that right? Maybe I should start visiting his garage more often—carrying a shotgun."

Gavin laughed and wrapped her slim figure in a conciliatory hug.

"Now, sweetheart, you know he's just teasing. There aren't any strange women hanging around my garage."

Jeanie smiled and winked at Melanie over Gavin's shoulder before he released her.

"Hi, Mom! Hi, Daddy! We're here." Sarah's cheery greeting interrupted them as she walked into the kitchen, trailed by Jesse, Trace, and his wife Lily.

For several moments, Melanie watched in fascination as the family milled around the kitchen in organized chaos, while the women instructed the men where to put the covered platters and iced cakes they'd brought. At last, like the efficient general she was, Jeanie shooed the men out of the kitchen, leaving the women alone in relative peace and quiet.

Sarah grinned impishly at Melanie's slightly stunned look and crossed to her side.

"Crazy, isn't it? You should see us on Christmas morning—it's an absolute zoo! How did Cole manage to talk you into enduring this?"

"He told me your mother made the best fried chicken in town," Melanie said with a smile. The words didn't begin to explain the forty-five minutes of cajoling he'd subjected her to before she'd given in and agreed to spend the afternoon with his family. She was still wary of any moves that spelled commitment, and meeting his family en masse was certainly in that category. Fortunately, it wasn't as if they were strangers. She'd grown to know them fairly well during the preparations for Sarah's wedding, and liked them all.

"Hi, Melanie."

Melanie looked up from the box of garter belts she was unpacking and sorting into drawers, and smiled with welcome at the two women crossing the Garden's polished floor toward her.

"Hi," she responded, her hands stilling over the blue ribbons and lace. "What are you two up to today?"

"Shopping," Sarah McFadden James answered and smiled sunnily, smoothing a palm over the round bulge of her tummy, "and eating lunch."

"That's all she does lately," Lily Townsend McFadden added wryly, eyeing Sarah's complacent look. "Eat and shop. Mostly eat!"

"That's because I'm eating for two," Sarah said with a virtuous air as she patted her stomach.

"How are you going to cope with your job and a baby at the same time, Sarah?" Melanie asked curiously.

"Jesse will help, and my Mom can't wait to spoil her, and me, rotten," Sarah laughed. "I probably won't be allowed to lift a finger."

"Trace and I will come over and spoil her, and then leave you to deal with her when she cries," Lily promised, mischief lighting the depths of her lavender eyes.

Sarah gave her sister-in-law a mock glare.

"Now *that* I believe—Trace still hasn't forgiven me for getting pregnant before you."

"That man!" Lily shook her head in affectionate disgust and looked at Melanie. "Do you know he actually wanted to race Jesse and Sarah to see who could have the first grandchild? I told him having babies is *not* a contest, but you know those McFadden brothers—the ultimate competitors!"

Melanie laughed and wondered fleetingly what Trace would have said if he'd known that Cole had already conceived the first McFadden grandchild. But the thought of their lost baby no longer caused the twist of pain she'd grown accustomed to over the years.

"My brother is a certifiable nut at times," Sarah said with a ladylike snort of disgust. "But to get back to the purpose of our visit, Melanie, we've come to take you away from work and out to lunch with us."

"Really?" Melanie was delightfully surprised. She'd become acquainted with Cole's sister Sarah when she coordinated the wedding arrangements for her and Jesse. She'd met Lily during those months also, because the beautiful brunette had been a bridesmaid for Sarah, and had fallen in love with Sarah's brother, Trace, at the same time. The three women had kept in touch in the months since and Melanie felt a genuine liking for the two sisters-in-law. *There's just something about those McFaddens*, she thought in passing. "I'd love to have lunch with you. Where are we going?"

"Suzanne's," Sarah answered promptly, naming a little homestyle restaurant a block away from Victoria's Garden on Main Street. "They have home-made pie on Tuesdays, and I've been dreaming about apple pie and ice cream ever since I woke up this morning."

Lily rolled her eyes at Melanie and laughed.

"I guess it's Suzanne's, then," she said with a shrug of acceptance. "You absolutely can't do anything with her when she's like this."

"Sounds good to me," Melanie said. "Just let me tell Mary Anne that I'm leaving—she's in the back unloading boxes and checking in merchandise."

She started toward the back of the shop, but before she rounded the end of the display counter the bell at the door jingled again and Cole stepped inside. As usual, the sight of him took her breath away and Melanie forgot Sarah and Lily's presence as he strode toward her.

"Hi, honey," he said and hugged her against him, bending to brush her mouth with his.

"Hi," she said, her voice throaty as she smiled up at him with her heart in her eyes.

"I've got some bad news," he frowned as his words wiped the smile from her lips and brought a wary caution springing to life in her green eyes.

"What is it?"

"I have to leave town for a few days. There are some problems with the new car and I have to fly back to Atlanta to check it out."

"Oh," Melanie's heart sank. "When are you leaving?"

"Tomorrow morning, but I have to make a lot of phone calls to suppliers and an engineering firm. I may not be able to take you out to dinner tonight."

"Can't you make the calls from my house?" she asked hopefully.

"I suppose so, but do you really want to spend the evening listening to me yelling at people over the phone?"

"Yes," she smiled up at him with relief. "Listening to you yell is better than not seeing you at all."

"All right—but you don't have to cook for me after working all day," he insisted. "I'll bring pizza with me." He bent to kiss her again.

"Pardon me," a voice said behind him, just as his lips brushed Melanie's, "but is there something you two would like to tell us?"

Startled, Cole looked over his shoulder to find Sarah and Lily watching him with raised eyebrows and barely concealed grins. He groaned and fixed them with a threatening glare.

"What are you two doing here?"

"We came by to take Melanie to lunch," his sister replied, "but that's neither here nor there. The real question is, what are *you* doing here?"

"I am here," Cole said without missing a beat, "to make arrangements to see my fiancée tonight."

Sarah's eyebrows shot skyward and her blue eyes widened with surprise and delight. Her startled glance shot to Melanie and noted with interest the red blush that colored her cheeks.

"Is he serious, Melanie? Are you two engaged?" she asked with excitement, blue eyes sparkling.

Melanie opened her mouth to deny Cole's words, but he forestalled her.

"I'm serious as I can be— but I haven't quite convinced Melanie yet," he grinned down at Melanie's pink face and slung an arm around her shoulder for a quick hug.

Lily watched the interplay between the two, as Cole winked at Melanie and she blushed a deeper shade of pink. But Melanie's usual cool reserve was absent and her body melted against Cole's with instinctive trust when he hugged her close. *Hmmm,* Lily thought speculatively. *I think I better warn Jeanie that another of her boys is going to have a wedding soon.* She smiled at the thought. Jeanie McFadden had been delighted when first Sarah and then Trace had married, and her dearest wish was that her other two sons, Cole and Josh, would follow their examples.

"Well, I'll leave you ladies to your lunch." Cole bent and brushed his mouth against Melanie's again in a quick kiss. "I'll see you tonight, sweetheart, about six o'clock."

"All right," Melanie nodded, and watched him leave before she steeled herself to face his sister and Lily. "I know you have questions," she said with a direct look, "but I don't have any answers. Not yet. As soon as I do, you'll be the first ones to know. After Cole, of course," she added.

Lily and Sarah exchanged a frustrated, speculative glance before looking back at Melanie's calmly determined face.

"All right," Lily answered for both her and Sarah, "we won't grill you—but I'm telling you right now, we expect a detailed accounting in the *very* near future.''

Melanie laughed. She couldn't help it, the look of determination on their two faces was identical. And she had no doubt that they meant what they said.

''All right—but for now, the subject of Cole McFadden and his alleged fiancée is off limits, okay?''

''Okay,'' Sarah said cheerfully. ''Now let's go get lunch, I'm starved!''

Melanie missed Cole so much it was terrifying. She was no longer a child, she told herself; she shouldn't feel his absence so deeply. She was a grown woman—she'd had a life before he came back into it, and she had a life now.

But it didn't matter how often she reminded herself that she'd always known he'd return to the east coast and his life there. Missing him was an ache that wouldn't leave her alone. Feeling miserable became a normal pattern as one week slipped into two, and then dragged on into three. Still, underlying the daily misery was a basic confidence in his promise to return. That confidence was bolstered by his almost daily telephone calls, and his continual assurance that he was just as miserable and impatient as she because of the work delays that kept him from returning to her on the next available flight.

Melanie kicked off her shoes and sank onto the floral cushion of the sofa in her living room with a deep sigh of relief.

"What a day," she said out loud, sipping iced tea from the moisture-beaded glass in her hand. The shop had been busier than usual, two of her most difficult customers had arrived together and proceeded to try on nearly everything in the shop before sailing out without purchasing a single item, and, worst of all, halfway through the afternoon the air conditioning had stopped working. Before she closed the door and locked it at five o'clock, the shop had been stifling.

She lifted her hair off her neck and leaned her head against the pillowed sofa back, closing her eyes in relief as she let the quiet coolness of the house enfold her while she listened to the muted sound of the six o'clock news.

". . . owner, Cole McFadden, who—"

Startled, Melanie lifted her head and sat upright, staring at the television set. A reporter was standing in the pits of a racetrack, talking into the microphone. She grabbed the remote control for the television and hit the volume, but she accidently hit the down button and the reporter's lips moved without sound. She muttered in frustration and reversed the volume.

". . . difficulties with the racing teams' car seem to be on their way to being solved with this afternoon's eastern seaboard win."

The camera panned to a shot of the winner's circle where Cole stood with his arm slung around a man Melanie didn't recognize. The picture was so clear it was as if he'd stepped into the room, and an unconscious answering smile curved her lips as she stared with helpless fascination at his handsome, dear face. The camera moved back to the reporter and for a moment, his toothpaste-ad smile obscured the image of Cole. Then, the camera angle shifted and once again Cole was visible over the reporter's shoulder.

The crowd noise increased as a beautiful blonde in a skin-tight T-shirt presented Cole with a huge silver trophy cup. Melanie's breath caught in her throat as the blonde pressed against him and kissed him, hotly, passionately. Never-endingly. Stunned, Melanie watched as the blonde finally released him and he grinned down at her, nodding and laughing as she went up on tiptoe to whisper in his ear.

". . . it looks as if the head of the McFadden Racing Team hasn't lost his touch, folks. I guess we know who Miss Motor Trend will be seeing tonight." The reporter's laugh echoed in Melanie's ears as she stared openmouthed at the busty blonde tucked under Cole's arm, while flashbulbs popped and the crowd roared.

The news program flashed back to the anchor team in the studio and Melanie hit the off button on the remote control, turning the television screen blessedly blank and silent.

"I don't believe this," she breathed out loud into the stillness of the empty house.

TEN

Was it a mistake?

No, this was no mistake, Melanie told herself, shock starting to wear off to be replaced by growing wrath. *Definitely not a mistake! I actually saw Cole with a beautiful blonde plastered against him, kissing her in front of thousands of cheering race fans and millions of television viewers across the United States! And furthermore, damn him, he looked like he was enjoying it!*

Her lashes narrowed as she stared at the darkened television screen. On top of the really rotten day she'd already had, Melanie was in no mood to give him the benefit of a doubt. What she really was in the mood for, she thought grimly, was to hit him over the head with one of her mother's cast-iron skillets.

She was no longer a heartbroken seventeen-year-old girl, willing to accept his actions without protest. She was a woman who had just seen her lover publicly kissing a scantily-clad beauty queen. There wasn't room for hurt and heartbreak. First, she was going to kill him! She'd worry about being heartbroken later. Much later.

Melanie snatched up the phone from its resting place on the glass-topped brass table at the end of the sofa and punched in a number.

"Julie? This is Melanie—I know it's after hours and I'm really sorry to call you at home, but I need to fly to Atlanta tomorrow. Can you make the reservations for me? What? No, no. No one is ill." *But someone may be dead by the time I'm through with him!* she thought with narrow-eyed determination. Julie's voice in her ear snapped her thoughts back to the conversation. "What's that? Oh, sure, I can run by your office and pick up the tickets in the morning. Thanks, Julie, you're an angel. 'Bye."

She hung up the phone and swept her shoes off the floor before stomping across the living room and up the stairs to her bedroom to pack.

She was halfway to the second story when the phone rang. She paused, one hand on the bannister, while she debated whether or not to answer it. It shrilled again, and then again.

"Oh, drat!" she muttered to herself and turned to retrace her steps. "I'm in no mood to chat with someone!"

She didn't hurry across the living room, almost hoping that whoever was calling would give up before she answered the phone. Unfortunately, it kept ringing. Whoever was calling her was determined to reach her. She snatched up the receiver and held it to her ear.

"Yes?" Her voice reflected her irritation.

"Melanie?" Her mother's voice said uncertainly.

"Yes, Mom, it's me."

"Oh, good," Angela said with relief. "For a minute there, I thought I'd reached a wrong number."

"No, Mom, you got me," Melanie said, some of her irritation disintegrating.

Angela didn't waste time with pleasantries. She got right to the purpose of her call.

"Did you watch the six o'clock news?"

Melanie closed her eyes and groaned silently.

"Yes, Mom, I did."

"Did you watch the sports segment?"

"Yes, Mom, I did."

Total silence gripped the line for a moment.

"Then you saw the report on Cole . . ."

"Yes, Mom, I saw the report on Cole."

"Well, for heaven's sakes," Angela said with frustration. She'd seen the buxom blonde throw her arms around Cole and glue her mouth to his, and had hoped against hope that Melanie had been detained at Victoria's Garden or hadn't turned her television on when she got home. It was obvious to her that Cole was the one being kissed and not the one doing the kissing. Unfortunately, she couldn't tell from Melanie's tone if her daughter had reached the same conclusion. "Are you upset?"

"Upset?" Melanie echoed. "Yes, mother, I think you could say I'm upset."

"Oh, dear, I was afraid of that," Angela said worriedly. "Now, Melanie, you shouldn't assume that he's being unfaithful. Just because that reporter made a sleazy comment about Cole doesn't mean it's true."

"I know that."

"And just because that woman grabbed him doesn't mean anything is going on there that shouldn't."

"I know—but you have to admit, Mom, he didn't act as if he objected!"

"No, that's true. But you shouldn't assume . . ." Angela paused. It suddenly occurred to her that Melanie's voice didn't hold the tear-filled devastation that she'd been worried she would hear. In fact, she sounded downright mad! "Melanie—just exactly how *do* you feel about this?"

"How do I feel?" Melanie stared at the cut-glass vase of fresh flowers centered on the glass and brass coffee table. If she didn't love that vase so much, she reflected, she'd throw it through the nearest window. "I think it's safe to say that I'm angry. No—make that irate. On second thought—make that raging, frothing-at-the-mouth furious!"

"Oh." Angela took a moment to digest that. Her mouth curved upward and bloomed into a full-fledged grin. "What are you going to do?"

"I'm going to catch the next plane to Atlanta and punch Cole McFadden right in the nose, that's what I'm going to do! If he thinks he's going to dump me for some busty blonde, he can think again! And after

I give him a broken nose, I just might give him a black eye!''

Angela laughed. ''Good for you! Well, I'm sure you have a lot to do if you're leaving town tomorrow, so I'll let you go. Take care, honey. Daddy and I will see you when you get back.''

''Right—I'll call you when I get back to town.''

Angela hung up the receiver and turned to her hovering husband, a delighted smile adding a warm sparkle to her eyes.

''Well? How is she?'' John Winters had only heard his wife's half of the conversation and still wasn't sure if Cole's latest escapade had plunged Melanie into despair.

''She's fine—actually, she's better than fine. She's going to fly to Atlanta tomorrow and punch Cole in the nose.''

John stared openmouthed at his grinning wife.

''Melanie? *Melanie* is going to fly halfway across the United States to punch somebody? Are we talking about the same person here? My daughter, who never even raises her voice and thinks losing one's temper is a symptom of sub-intelligence? What happened to her?''

''She's in love,'' Angela said happily. ''And whether she realizes it or not, she's finally found something worth fighting for. I hope Cole is ready to get married, because ready or not, I'm sure Melanie won't settle for anything else!''

Melanie hung up the receiver and started back up the stairs. She reached the halfway point when the phone shrilled again.

"Oh, no," she groaned and half-turned to glare at the offending instrument. She willed it to stop ringing, but it defied her. She threw a suffering glance upward and retraced her steps.

"Yes?" Her voice held the same impatience it had earlier.

"Melanie?" Sarah's voice sounded in her ear. "Is that you?"

"Yes, this is me," Melanie answered cautiously, unsure if she wanted to talk to Cole's sister.

"Oh, good. For a moment, I thought I had a wrong number—your voice sounds different. Are you all right?"

Melanie closed her eyes and took a deep breath before answering.

"Yes—I'm fine. How are you?"

"Oh, I'm fine." Sarah brushed aside Melanie's polite inquiry and got to the crux of her call. "Did you watch the news tonight?"

Oh, no, Melanie groaned silently. *Here we go again!*

"Yes, I did." she answered, her voice carefully neutral.

"Then you saw Cole?" Sarah asked.

"Yes, I saw Cole."

"Oh." Sarah paused for a moment while she considered how to proceed. Melanie wasn't making this easy. "I just wanted to call and tell you I'm sure that disgusting comment the reporter made wasn't true. Cole is crazy about you, Melanie. He'd never risk his future with you for a fling with some blonde bimbo!"

"You don't think so?"

"I know so!" Sarah said emphatically. "You don't think so, either, do you?"

"I'm not sure what to think," Melanie said with blunt honesty. "But I do know that I'm furious with him."

"You are?" *Uh-oh!* "What are you going to do?" she asked worriedly.

"I'm going to fly to Atlanta tomorrow and choke him—after I punch him several times." Her voice held a purr of anticipation.

"You are?" Sarah felt like a parrot. She could hardly believe that Melanie was considering clobbering her big brother. In all the time she'd known Melanie, Sarah had never seen her serene calm so much as shaken. Now, she was contemplating physical violence? *Wow*, she thought with dawning realization, *she must really be crazy about Cole!* "Well, in that case, I'll let you go. I'm sure you have a lot to get done if you're leaving town tomorrow. 'Bye, Melanie. Tell Cole hi for me."

"I'll do that. 'Bye."

Melanie hung up the receiver once again and stood staring at it for a long moment, a perplexed frown creasing her brow. Both her mother and Sarah had seemed relieved and even glad that she was so mad at Cole. Why? No satisfactory answer came to mind, and with a shrug she started back up the stairs.

She'd reached the exact same step halfway up the stairs when the phone rang again.

"Oh, for Pete's sake!" she said out loud, shooting a vexed glare at it. It rang demandingly again, and with a final disgusted look, Melanie turned her back on it and continued up the stairs. *It's probably my mother again, or someone else who saw the news and wants to know how I feel about it. I don't have time to reassure one more person that I'm not ready to commit suicide. Murder—yes—but definitely not suicide!*

"Hey, Cole, way to go!" Bobby McAllister flashed him a grin and a thumbs-up sign.

"Thanks, Bobby."

"Yeah," Kyle Dennison chimed in. "Congratulations on both wins—the Trenton Five Hundred and Miss Motor Trend!"

Cole groaned and didn't answer as he loped up the steps to his second-floor office. He flung himself into the upholstered leather chair behind his desk and dialed Melanie's number in CastleRock. He counted an even dozen rings before he gave up and dropped the receiver back into its cradle.

"Damn it," he growled out loud, and picked up the receiver to punch the numbers once again.

"Good morning, Victoria's Garden," the feminine voice said over the line, "May I help you?"

"Hello, Mary Anne, this is Cole again. Has Melanie called in yet?"

"Hello, Cole. No, I'm sorry, she hasn't. I haven't heard from her since she called me at home last night and asked me to take over the Garden for the next few days."

"She didn't say anything about why? Or if she was leaving town—or wasn't feeling well?"

"I'm sure she was feeling fine—she sounded perfectly healthy. She probably just wanted a few days to relax," Mary Anne said soothingly, just as she had during Cole's last three telephone calls. "I promise I'll tell her to call you the moment I hear from her."

"All right, thanks, Mary Anne."

" 'Bye, Cole."

" 'Bye." With a frustrated grunt of annoyance, Cole dropped his receiver back into its cradle. "Damn it, where is she?" He thrust his fingers through his hair, ruffling the tawny mane even more. He'd started calling her house shortly after he'd seen the sports report on national news the night before. At first he'd gotten a busy signal, and then the phone simply rang and rang, with no answer. He was about ready to board a plane and fly home to make sure she was okay, work or no work.

The phone rang and he grabbed it, but it was a delinquent supplier. Disappointed and frustrated, Cole propped his booted feet on the edge of his desk and leaned back in his chair while he listened with growing irritation to the man's excuses.

Melanie handed the fare to the cabbie and stepped out onto the curb. The late afternoon sun was hot and the humidity had curled little tendrils of black silk at her temples, although the rest of her long hair was still confined in the intricate weaving of a French braid from her crown to her nape. The building facing her was two stories, its plain white-painted walls decorated only by a modest sign in block letters, which spelled out *McFadden Racing Enterprises*.

She smoothed her palms down her hips and over the pencil-straight skirt of her white suit, slung the strap of her purse over her shoulder, and bent to pick up the small leather overnight bag at her feet. She crossed the sidewalk, pushed open the door under the entrance sign, and stepped inside.

The small office she entered was empty. Two leather-covered chairs and a matching black sofa were placed against two walls and faced a secretary's desk and filing cabinets. File folders and papers were stacked on top of the desk and piled next to the computer screen and keyboard on the long table behind the desk.

Melanie waited, but no one appeared. A door stood ajar just beyond the end of the sofa in the far left corner of the square room. The sounds of men's voices were interspersed with music and chatter from a radio, and the clatter of tools and hum of machines.

"Hello? Hello?" She tried several times to elicit a response, but no inquiring face popped through the door to answer her.

She didn't have the patience to wait long. The short hours since she'd seen Cole on the six o'clock news hadn't been long enough to dampen her anger. She dropped the briefcase-style overnight bag on the sofa, squared her shoulders, and crossed the short span of office carpet to push the half-open inner door wider.

The garage area before her was spacious and well lit. Some eight to twelve men were busy working in the wide space, five of them bent over an engine sitting on a freestanding work table in the center of the room. The electric-blue car body, covered with brilliant-colored decals naming the racing team's sponsors, was completely removed from the chassis and sat in a corner in lonely splendor. State-of-the-art tools and equipment hung on the wall above a long workbench, and country-western music was piped into the room through speakers hung in the corners.

"Hey, Jerry," Bobby nudged the older mechanic overseeing the engine work.

"Yeah," Jerry answered absently as he kept an eagle eye on an apprentice mechanic's work. "What is it?"

"We got company."

"Huh?" Jerry frowned and glanced up. "Where?"

"At the office door."

Jerry looked over his shoulder and went perfectly still, his square jaw dropping as he saw Melanie.

"Well, I'll be damned," he whistled softly as he straightened and absentmindedly caught up a rag to wipe his hands on.

"Yeah, me, too," Bobby grinned in agreement as his appreciative stare ran over the green-eyed brunette's curves in the conservative white suit. "Classy, huh? Who is she?"

"*That,*" Jerry said with a grin, "is Cole's woman."

"She is?" Bobby looked again. "I thought the

flavor of the week was blonde, as in Miss Motor Trend."

"Nope, not a chance. Unless I'm way off base, that's Melanie Winters and she's been Cole's obsession for eight years."

"You're kidding!" Bobby stared, intrigued. But Jerry didn't answer him because he was striding across the concrete garage floor toward the beautiful brunette.

Melanie was aware that the dozen men in the garage had quit working and were making no effort to disguise their curiosity as they stared at her. She saw a young mechanic elbow an older man, whose brown hair was threaded with gray, and felt a surge of relief when he looked up, smiled, and walked toward her, wiping his hands on a red rag.

"Hello there." A wide smile wreathed his face and lit his brown eyes. "Unless I'm dead wrong, my guess is that your name is Melanie."

"You're right." Melanie was taken aback, and for a moment forgot she meant to ask him where she could find Cole. "How did you know?"

The stocky, older man chuckled.

"I've been with Cole ever since he got his first driving contract. He's carried a picture of you in his wallet ever since he was a kid."

Startled into speechlessness, Melanie's wide green eyes searched his, but the brown eyes that smiled back at her held a complete lack of guile.

"I reckon you're lookin' for Cole, aren't you?" he asked.

"Yes," she said firmly, reminded of why she was here. "I am. Is he here?"

"Yup, got here about half an hour ago. He's up in his office."

"Up in his office?" Melanie repeated questioningly, her gaze lifting to find a balcony that ran along the wall behind her.

"Yeah, just go up those stairs and it's the first door you come to," Jerry instructed, lifting a calloused, greasy hand to point to a metal stairway to their left.

"Thanks." Melanie gave him a perfunctory smile and turned away to the stairs.

Twelve pairs of male eyes lit with appreciation as they watched her climb the stairs, long legs clad in silk hose, displayed to advantage beneath the short hem of her skirt.

Melanie lifted her hand and rapped her knuckles against the door panel.

"Yeah—come in, it's open," Cole's voice growled from beyond the door.

Melanie turned the knob, pushed open the door, and stepped inside. Cole was talking on the phone, the receiver cradled between his shoulder and ear, a sheaf of papers held in his hands. His long legs were stretched out with his feet crossed at the ankles and propped on the edge of his desk. He didn't look up when she entered, and she stood there for a moment while he listened intently and with obvious growing irritation to whoever was on the other end of the line.

She didn't have time to put up with him ignoring

her. She gave the door a hard push and it slammed behind her. The resulting crash brought Cole's head up. His eyes widened in surprise when he saw her and his feet hit the floor with a thud.

"Call me later, Kenny," he said abruptly and slammed the receiver back into its cradle. He surged out of his chair and strode around the end of his desk toward her. "Melanie, thank God!" A smile of relief and delight wreathed his face and lit his eyes. He reached for her, but she stepped back and planted a small fist against his chest to stop him.

"Melanie?" Cole looked down at the little hand against his shirt front in confusion. "Is something wrong?"

"Wrong?" she repeated, lashes narrowing over her eyes. "Yes, I think you may safely assume that something is *wrong*."

"Uh-oh." Warily, Cole took another look at her. She was so angry she fairly sizzled with it. Her green eyes were shooting dark emerald sparks, and he could almost see the crackle and snap of electric fury. "Something tells me that you saw that idiot reporter on television last night."

"I didn't think that sleazy reporter was nearly as idiotic as that sleazy blonde you were glued against!"

"Now, Melanie, I can explain . . ." He began, but she cut him off with an impatient snarl.

"I don't want to hear your explanation. I didn't fly all the way from Iowa to Georgia to hear some trumped up excuse for your behavior!"

"Why did you fly all the way to Georgia?" Cole

asked in bemusement. He'd love to tell her that she was heart-stoppingly beautiful when she was angry. But fortunately, he had enough sense not to say it out loud.

"I flew here to tell you all the ways I plan to kill you," Melanie said angrily. "History is *not* repeating itself, McFadden! You are not dumping me again, *especially* not for some Miss Motor and Tires!"

"Miss Motor Trend," Cole corrected her, trying to restrain the grin that tugged at the corners of his mouth.

"Whatever," Melanie said impatiently, waving her hand in dismissal. "The point here is that we aren't doing this again!" One pink-tipped finger tapped his chest and he took a step backward for each stabbing motion. "You don't have the excuse of being a rookie driver who's tempted to sample all the side benefits of fame that come your way! And I absolutely refuse to put up with your kissing other women—on television or off! Do you hear me?"

"Yes, ma'am," he said with solemn meekness while he struggled and lost the fight to keep a wide grin from breaking across his face.

"And furthermore," Melanie paused to eye him suspiciously. "What's so funny? This is no laughing matter, Cole. I am going to tear you limb from limb, not to mention bruise your face and break your nose if you don't behave yourself! What *are* you laughing about?" she broke off to demand as he burst into delighted laughter.

"I'm sorry, honey," he said with a choked laugh, "but you're so damn cute when you're mad."

It was the wrong thing to say. Melanie's temperature skyrocketed and the green glare she fixed on him was lethal. She lifted her hand to slug him and he ducked and caught it in his, bending her arm gently behind her back and wrapping his other arm around her to pin her free arm to her side.

She struggled, but he held her easily.

"I hate you, Cole McFadden," she snapped at him, her face flushed and her green eyes filled with fury.

"No, you don't," he said with confidence. "And now that we've got that settled, you're going to listen to the apology I've been trying to give you since I saw that damn news report last night. Melanie, I didn't kiss her, she kissed me. The sponsor told her to do it and short of making a scene on national television, I couldn't get out of it. I don't even know Miss Motor Trend's name—I never saw her before the race yesterday and I haven't seen her since. It was strictly for publicity, I swear."

"That's not what the news reporter said!"

'If I ever get my hands on that reporter, I'm going to kill him," Cole muttered in exasperation. "Honey, I swear to you—I never saw that woman before yesterday!"

"What about after?" Melanie lifted a skeptical brow at him.

"After what?"

"After the race. Did you see her last night?"

"No, Melanie," Cole said with patience. His blue

gaze pinned hers, reading the disbelief that still lurked in the depths of her green eyes. Her face was flushed with color, her eyes brilliant emerald gems beneath ebony brows. "You must be out of your mind, if you think I'd jeopardize my love for you with any other woman."

"But she was beautiful."

"So? Have you looked in a mirror lately? I've never met a woman who could hold a candle to you, honey."

"Hmmm," she murmured, mollified, her lashes dropping to shield her eyes. She tugged her arm free from under his and lifted slim fingers to toy with the top button of his shirt.

She didn't say anything further and Cole ducked his chin in an effort to look into her eyes.

"So, are you still mad at me?" he asked.

"I'm not sure—I'm thinking about it."

"Well, while you're considering it, why don't you kiss me hello?" he said huskily, and was rewarded by a slight tilting of her chin that allowed his mouth to reach hers. Cole took full advantage of the opportunity and it was several long moments before he lifted his head to breathe. "You know, I'm kinda glad you misunderstood that publicity stunt."

Startled, Melanie lifted her head from where she snuggled against his chest and looked up at him.

"Why?"

"Because," he said with a trace of smug confidence, "you must really love me a lot to fly all the way from Iowa to Georgia just to yell at me."

"What?" She stared at him as if he'd lost his

mind. ‘‘You’re crazy, McFadden. What kind of women have you been seeing that make you think a desire to kill you is proof of love?’’

‘‘You must have felt something powerful to come all this way—even if it was to kill me,’’ he argued with irrefutable logic.

‘‘Yes—a desire to inflict bodily harm,’’ she snapped back.

‘‘Yup,’’ he nodded his head in satisfaction. ‘‘That’s love.’’

‘‘No, that’s mayhem and murder!’’

‘‘Nope, that’s love. If all you wanted was revenge, you would have waited and plotted. But you didn’t, you raced across the country to claim what was yours—namely, me.’’

‘‘That’s ridicu—’’ Melanie’s brows knit as she considered the possibility that he was right.

Cole saw the frown that creased a tiny vee between her eyebrows and knew she’d gone from absolute denial to considering the possibility that he might be right.

He waited without speaking, watching her face. And he knew the instant she realized he was right by the stunned awe that darkened her eyes.

‘‘Cole,’’ she said, her voice throaty with shock and need.

‘‘What, honey?’’ he said with tender gentleness.

‘‘I think I . . .’’

Behind her, the door swung abruptly inward and a middle-aged woman in slacks and a tailored white blouse, glasses perched on the end of her nose and a pencil thrust into the cropped blonde hair above her ear, walked briskly into the office.

"Cole, I have to ask you about the files—oops, am I interrupting something?"

"Yes, you are, Theresa, but since you're here, ask me." Cole said. Melanie shifted to move out of his arms, but he clasped his hands together at the small of her back and refused to release her.

Theresa's bright gaze moved shrewdly from her boss to the blushing woman in his arms and quickly analyzed the situation.

"Sorry—I'll be brief. I've separated and had the movers pack all of the files I'm sure will be going with us, and I've made a stack of the files I'm not sure about. I need to have you go over the list and check off which ones are to be packed immediately and sent to the CastleRock office, and which ones you want to remain here."

"All right, Theresa, read the list out loud and I'll tell you yes or no," Cole said. He leaned back, settling his hips against the edge of the desk, his arms wrapped around Melanie's slim waist to keep her with him.

Melanie tried unobtrusively to move out of his arms, but he only tightened his grip.

"Hold still," he murmured against her hair, and returned his attention to Theresa.

Melanie listened with growing bewilderment as Cole and his secretary worked quickly and efficiently to narrow the list of files to be moved immediately. At last, they finished and Theresa moved briskly out of the office, closing the door behind her.

Cole looked down into Melanie's face and read the confusion and hope on her expressive features.

"Don't you have something you'd like to ask me?" he said with a lazy smile, his hands linked at her waist.

"Yes," she said, her gaze fixed on his. "Are you moving your office to CastleRock?"

"Yes, I am."

"Why?" She held her breath, afraid to believe what she suspected.

"Because I'm going to be semi-retired, at least from driving. I'm going to keep the design-engineering and car-building part of the team. I'm going to move back to CastleRock and build my house on the lake. And, if I'm very lucky, fill it with laughter and children."

"Really?" Melanie's voice was husky with emotion.

"Yes, really. How many kids would you like?"

"Do I get to make them with you?" she asked, and read his answer in the leap of blue fire in his eyes.

"Oh, yeah," he breathed. "That's one of the best parts, the fun of trying. Will you marry me, Melanie?"

And she burst into tears.

Cole was dumbfounded. Tears were not the reaction he'd expected. Worse yet, she was crying and trying to talk at the same time, her face buried in his shirt front while her hands gripped fistfuls of the cotton.

"Melanie?" he said anxiously, but she only hiccuped and cried harder. "Damn it, honey, you're scaring me to death! Don't you want to get married?

If you don't want to, then just live with me. I don't care how I get to have you, I just want you with me! Honey . . . ?''

Melanie lifted her head and smiled at him through her tears, her face glowing with a beauty that took his breath away.

''I love you, and I want to marry you, and make babies with you, and . . .'' She reached up and slipped her hands around his neck to tug his mouth down to hers.

''Damn,'' Cole groaned a few minutes later when they both had to come up for air. ''This office isn't the best place for making love—I don't even have a sofa.''

Melanie's green eyes laughed at his look of frustration.

''There's always the top of your desk,'' she teased.

''Now, there's a thought,'' he responded and swept a forearm across the desk, scattering papers and files over the floor.

Melanie shrieked and giggled when he caught her waist and picked her up.

''No, wait! I was kidding!''

''I'm not.'' Fire flickered beneath the amusement in his eyes.

''Then let's go to your place,'' she suggested.

''All right,'' he agreed reluctantly. ''I'll try to hold out that long.''

''How far away is your apartment?'' she asked with sudden concern.

''Fifteen minutes—maybe twenty, depending on traffic.''

"That is a long time," she said.

"There's always the desk. Sure you won't reconsider?"

"No, and you know very well you're teasing."

"Yeah, you're right," he said ruefully. "For a variety of reasons, not least of which is that I'm sure the whole crew is holding their breath downstairs and taking bets on what's going on up here."

Melanie blushed, horrified as she remembered how she'd yelled at him earlier.

"Oh, my goodness! I'm sure they heard every word I said!"

"Not the important stuff," Cole said, his expression gentling as his gaze ran over her face. He tugged her back into his arms. "Tell me again," he urged gruffly.

"Tell you what," she said softly, her nose nearly touching his, his lips a tempting breath away.

"You know what," he said with sudden fierceness. "I've dreamed of you saying it, Melanie. Tell me."

"I love you," she murmured against his mouth. "I've always loved you. I was just afraid to say it again—I never stopped loving you."

And with a sureness that this time their love was safe forever, she lifted her lips that fraction of an inch and sealed his mouth with hers. His arms tightened around her with satisfying solidity, echoing his unspoken promise to hold her tight through all the long years of love and laughter ahead of them.

SHARE THE FUN . . .
SHARE YOUR NEW-FOUND TREASURE!!

You don't want to let your new books out of your sight? That's okay. Your friends can get their own. Order below.

No. 15 A MATTER OF TIME by Ann Bullard
Does Josh *really* want Christine or is there something else?

No. 16 FACE TO FACE by Shirley Faye
Christi's definitely not Damon's type. So, what's the attraction?

No. 17 OPENING ACT by Ann Patrick
Big city playwright meets small town sheriff and life heats up.

No. 18 RAINBOW WISHES by Jacqueline Case
Mason is looking for more from life. Evie may be his pot of gold!

No. 19 SUNDAY DRIVER by Valerie Kane
Carrie breaks through all Cam's defenses showing him how to love.

No. 20 CHEATED HEARTS by Karen Lawton Barrett
T.C. and Lucas find their way back into each other's hearts.

No. 22 NEVER LET GO by Laura Phillips
Ryan has a big dilemma. Kelly is the answer to *all* his prayers.

- -

Meteor Publishing Corporation
Dept. 492, P. O. Box 41820, Philadelphia, PA 19101-9828

Please send the books I've indicated below. Check or money order only—no cash, stamps or C.O.D.s (PA residents, add 6% sales tax). I am enclosing $2.95 plus 75¢ handling fee for *each* book ordered.

Total Amount Enclosed: $__________.

___ No. 4	___ No. 3	___ No. 10	___ No. 16
___ No. 21	___ No. 5	___ No. 11	___ No. 17
___ No. 70	___ No. 6	___ No. 12	___ No. 18
___ No. 88	___ No. 7	___ No. 13	___ No. 19
___ No. 1	___ No. 8	___ No. 14	___ No. 20
___ No. 2	___ No. 9	___ No. 15	___ No. 22

Please Print:
Name ______________________________
Address ______________________ Apt. No. ______
City/State ____________________ Zip ______

Allow four to six weeks for delivery. Quantities limited.